W9-AQJ-113

Who's Your Daddy?

Clint woke up the next morning and realized the boy was standing by him, hitting him on the head with the flat of his hand.

"Okay, okay," Clint said. "I'm up."

He sat up and looked at the boy, who—amazingly—smiled at him.

"Do you have a name?"

The boy scrunched up his face.

"Can you say anything?" Clint asked.

"Mama," the boy said.

"Well, that's a start."

This time Clint heated the remainder of the beans before feeding them to the boy. He had no coffee for himself, though, because they had not camped near water, and he didn't want to use the water in his canteen, preferring to save it for the boy. So he ate the rest of the jerky for his own breakfast.

The fire had apparently kept the boy warm enough overnight, because he had not stirred once. Of course, that could have been because he was so exhausted.

The boy seemed to enjoy the warm beans and drank plenty of water.

"Okay," Clint said, putting him back on the blanket, "wait there while I saddle up."

By the time he finished saddling Eclipse, the boy had walked several yards, once again with that determined little march of his.

"Oh no," Clint said, scooping him up, "not again. We're going for a ride."

He sniffed the boy's bottom, was surprised to find that he hadn't soiled himself again—yet.

DON'T MISS THESE
ALL-ACTION WESTERN SERIES
FROM THE BERKLEY PUBLISHING GROUP

THE GUNSMITH by J. R. Roberts

Clint Adams was a legend among lawmen, outlaws, and ladies. They called him . . . the Gunsmith.

LONGARM by Tabor Evans

The popular long-running series about Deputy U.S. Marshal Custis Long—his life, his loves, his fight for justice.

SLOCUM by Jake Logan

Today's longest-running action Western. John Slocum rides a deadly trail of hot blood and cold steel.

BUSHWHACKERS by B. J. Lanagan

An action-packed series by the creators of Longarm! The rousing adventures of the most brutal gang of cutthroats ever assembled—Quantrill's Raiders.

DIAMONDBACK by Guy Brewer

Dex Yancey is Diamondback, a Southern gentleman turned con man when his brother cheats him out of the family fortune. Ladies love him. Gamblers hate him. But nobody pulls one over on Dex . . .

WILDGUN by Jack Hanson

The blazing adventures of mountain man Will Barlow—from the creators of Longarm!

TEXAS TRACKER by Tom Calhoun

J.T. Law: the most relentless—and dangerous—manhunter in all Texas. Where sheriffs and posses fail, he's the best man to bring in the most vicious outlaws—for a price.

THE GUNSMITH

399

DEATH IN THE FAMILY

J. R. ROBERTS

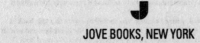

JOVE BOOKS, NEW YORK

THE BERKLEY PUBLISHING GROUP
Published by the Penguin Group
Penguin Group (USA) LLC
375 Hudson Street, New York, New York 10014

USA • Canada • UK • Ireland • Australia • New Zealand • India • South Africa • China

penguin.com

A Penguin Random House Company

DEATH IN THE FAMILY

A Jove Book / published by arrangement with the author

For information, address: The Berkley Publishing Group,
a division of Penguin Group (USA) LLC,
375 Hudson Street, New York, New York 10014.

ISBN: 978-0-515-15551-8

PUBLISHING HISTORY
Jove mass-market edition / March 2015

PRINTED IN THE UNITED STATES OF AMERICA

10 9 8 7 6 5 4 3 2 1

Cover illustration by Sergio Giovine.

ONE

Clint Adams couldn't believe his eyes.

He'd seen a lot of things in his life on the trail, but this was something new.

It started as just a glimpse of something moving in the Wyoming distance, something small. At first he thought it was a small animal, maybe a coyote. He intended to skirt around it, so as not to spook it, but the he realized his mistake. It wasn't a coyote at all—or any kind of animal, for that matter.

It was a child.

As he got closer, he saw that it was a toddler, just walking along, occasionally tripping and almost falling, but holding its hands out and catching its balance at the last minute.

Closer still and he could see that it was a boy, and that he was still in a diaper. His chubby little legs were just pumping along, and when Clint could see his face, the boy wore a very determined expression.

Clint dismounted and approached the boy, who never looked up and never stopped walking. His arms, legs, and face were covered with dirt, so he must have been out there for a good while. Clint looked around, couldn't see any houses or wagons in any direction. He wondered how far the boy had come, and what the heck he was doing out there.

Finally, Clint decided to stop him. He stepped in front of him and crouched down. As he approached, the boy finally looked up and saw Clint, but he didn't stop walking even then until he walked into Clint's hands.

"Hey, buddy," Clint said. "How are ya doing?"

The boy frowned. Clint wasn't good at guessing children's ages, but the fact that he was still in a diaper had to make him under two.

Suddenly, looking into the boy's eyes, he could see how tired the child was. And at that moment, the boy started to cry.

Clint stood, picking the child up and taking him with him. The tears made tracks in the dirt on his face.

"You must be starving and thirsty," Clint said. Luckily, it was fall and the sun wasn't beating down as relentlessly as it might have been.

"Come on," Clint said, "let's see if we've got anything for you to eat."

He carried the child back to Eclipse. At the very least he could give the boy some water. He uncapped his canteen with his teeth, held it to the boy's mouth, and the tot stopped crying long enough to drink greedily.

"That's enough," Clint said, taking the canteen away. "You don't want to get sick."

The boy started crying again, and Clint could smell the stench coming from the diaper.

"Good God," he said, "you need to be cleaned and changed and fed, and that's just not something I'm real good at, but we're going to have to give it a go."

It was early and there was still plenty of travel time, but he decided to camp right where he was and see what he could do to make the boy more comfortable.

"Well, Eclipse," he said to the big Darley, "looks like you and me got some babysitting to do."

Clint spread a blanket on the ground, then his bedroll, then put the boy down on it. He tore a shirt up into strips so he could use one part as a diaper and another to clean the boy with. First he wiped off the feces and urine, then tied a clean strip around him as a diaper. He used a third strip to wash the boy's face, hands, arms, and legs.

After that, he looked through his saddlebags for something the boy could eat, but all he had was some beef jerky and a can of beans. The boy would not be able to chew the jerky, so Clint opened the can of beans and fed them to the boy cold, a bean at a time. The boy appreciated the food and kept opening his mouth for more.

"I wonder," Clint said while he was feeding him, "can you talk at all at your age? Can you say any words?"

The boy was too busy eating to even try. Clint stopped feeding him before the boy was ready, gave him some water to wash it down. Too many beans might cause the boy to soil his makeshift diaper too soon. Clint was hoping he'd be able to find a house, a wagon, or a town the next day before he was forced to figure something out about a diaper again.

The boy complained for a while, wanting more to eat. Clint checked his bare feet, found a few cuts that he was able to clean, but they didn't seem to be causing the boy too much discomfort. Most of it seemed to be from the fact that he was still hungry. Eventually, though, he was overcome by fatigue, and he fell asleep. Clint actually wrapped him in the blanket, so that when the night cooled a bit, the boy wouldn't be too cold.

Clint built a fire, but ate some of the beans cold with beef jerky—leaving just a little that he'd be able to feed the boy in the morning—drank some water, then took the time to unsaddle Eclipse for the night. He let the animal feed on some brush, and tried to make himself comfortable against his saddle. He had given the boy his bedroll and blanket, so he folded his arms across his chest, hoping the night wouldn't get too cold.

He had several theories about the boy. He'd wandered off from either a house or a wagon, possibly one that had been hit by outlaws or Indians. Clint didn't know how far he'd walked, but it couldn't have been that far, or his bare feet would have been in even worse shape. He felt fairly certain he'd find the answers in the morning.

He just hoped the boy would sleep through the night.

TWO

Clint woke up the next morning and realized the boy was standing by him, hitting him on the head with the flat of his hand.

"Okay, okay," Clint said, "I'm up."

He sat up and looked at the boy, who—amazingly—smiled at him.

"Do you have a name?"

The boy scrunched up his face.

"Can you say anything?" Clint asked.

"Mama," the boy said.

"Well, that's a start."

This time Clint heated the remainder of the beans before feeding them to the boy. He had no coffee for himself, though, because they had not camped near water, and he didn't want to use the water in his canteen, preferring to save it for the boy. So he ate the rest of the jerky for his own breakfast.

The fire had apparently kept the boy warm enough overnight, because he had not stirred once. Of course, that could have been because he was so exhausted.

The boy seemed to enjoy the warm beans and drank plenty of water.

"Okay," Clint said, putting him back on the blanket, "wait there while I saddle up."

By the time he finished saddling Eclipse, the boy had walked several yards, once again with that determined little march of his.

"Oh no," Clint said, scooping him up, "not again. We're going for a ride."

He sniffed the boy's bottom, was surprised to find that he hadn't soiled himself again—yet.

He mounted Eclipse, holding the boy in one arm, then sat the boy just in front of him.

"We're going to go and find your mama," he said.

"Mama," the boy said.

"Right."

"Hi."

"Right," Clint said, "hi."

He gigged Eclipse with his heels and they started off in an easterly direction.

Fairly quickly Clint came to a sign that said CHESTER, WYOMING, 3 MI.

He looked down at the top of the boy's head.

"Could you have walked three miles?"

The boy grabbed a handful of Eclipse's mane and pulled it.

"I don't think so," Clint said, "but let's find out."

He urged Eclipse on, toward Chester.

As Clint rode into the town of Chester with a baby in front of him, he drew curious looks from the people walking up and down the streets.

It was obviously an election year. VOTE FOR LENNON signs and placards were posted all up and down the main street, in the windows of shops and restaurants.

The only thing Clint didn't see were signs stating who the other candidate was.

By the time he reached the sheriff's office and dismounted, he had drawn a crowd.

"Anybody know who this little boy is?" he asked, holding the kid up.

Nobody answered, but somebody called out, "Who are you?"

He lowered the boy and said, "One answer at a time."

He turned and stepped to the office door, opened it, and entered, still holding the boy in one arm—his left. He made sure his right hand—his gun hand—was free.

As he entered, a man looked up from his broom and stared at him. He looked like a drunk swamping out a saloon, his clothes and hair disheveled, but he was wearing a badge on his dirty shirt.

"Help ya?" he asked.

Clint thought this swamper had put the sheriff's badge on because nobody had been around.

"I'm looking for the sheriff."

"You found him." The man stopped sweeping and leaned on the broom.

"You?"

"Yeah, that's right." He set the broom aside now, walked to the desk, and sat down. "I had a hard night. What can I do for you?"

Clint thought this man looked as if he'd had a hard life, not just a hard night.

"I found this child wandering around alone outside of town," Clint said. "He was hungry, tired, and barefoot. Do you know him?"

The sheriff leaned forward and peered at the boy.

"Can't say that I do," the man said. "Why'd you bring him to Chester?"

"Because it was the first town I came to," Clint said.

"Sorry," the man said, "but I can't help you. These kids all look alike to me."

"So nobody in town came to you about a missing baby?" Clint asked.

"Nope," the sheriff said. "Nobody."

"Well," Clint said, "can I leave him with you? I don't—"

"Jesus, no!" the sheriff said, jumping to his feet. "I ain't gonna take him. This is no place for a baby!"

"But he needs a bath, and he needs changing again," Clint said, wrinkling his nose. The stench had started just outside of town. It was remarkable that the boy wasn't bawling his head off. "I can't keep him."

"You found him," the sheriff said. "You find somebody to take him."

"Where would you suggest?"

The sheriff thought a moment, then said, "Try the cat-house."

"You want me to take him to a whorehouse?"

"Well," the sheriff said, "there's women there. One of them should know how to take care of a child."

Clint stared at the man for a moment, then asked, "What's your name, Sheriff?"

"Murphy," the man said. "Tom Murphy. Why?"

"Because, Tom Murphy," Clint said, "you might just be a genius."

THREE

Clint found out from the sheriff where the whorehouse was, and stepped out of the sheriff's office to find most of the crowd still there.

"Whose baby is that?" a woman shouted.

"Who are you?" a man called out.

"Where did you get the baby?"

Clint mounted Eclipse, turned him, and forced his way through the crowd.

"If you want your questions answered," he called out, "go talk to the sheriff!"

He rode off up the street, following the sheriff's directions to the whorehouse.

Maddy's Cathouse was just on the edge of town, almost over the boundary line. In fact, the sheriff told him it was once out of town, until the boundaries were changed so the town could tax the place.

He reined in Eclipse in front of the building and dismounted, still holding the baby in his left arm.

"Okay, kid," he said to the baby, "let's see if we can find someplace to leave you."

He went up the steps and knocked on the heavy oak door. Unlike most whorehouses he'd been to, the door was not answered by a scantily clad woman, but by a fully dressed man. He was tall, broad-shouldered, clean-shaven, in his late twenties. His clothes were clean, looked new, and he wasn't wearing a gun.

"Help ya?" he asked.

"Yes," Clint said, "I'd like to speak to the lady of the house."

"You kiddin'?" he asked. "There's lots of girls in this house, but no ladies."

"Then I'll take the madam."

"What's with the kid?"

"I found him."

"Where?"

"That's what I want to talk to the madam about."

"You think it's hers?" he asked Clint. "Or one of the girls here?"

"I don't know whose it is," Clint said, "but I need to leave it someplace until I find out."

"And you wanna leave it here?" the man asked. "You know what kind of place this is?"

"I do," Clint said. "That's why I asked to see the madam."

The man shook his head. "She ain't gonna wanna—"

"How about you let her decide for herself?" Clint said, cutting him off.

"Yeah, okay," the man said finally, "wait here."

"Come in," Lily Carter called.

Andy Cardwell opened the door and entered his boss's office.

"What is it?" she asked.

"There's a man at the door asking for you."

"Is that unusual?" she asked. "There's always men at the door."

"Well . . ."

"Well what?" She was in her mid-forties, still looked good enough to be working, if she wanted to. But she was also a hard woman, always in charge. Cardwell was her security, and warmed her bed when she wanted it.

"Well . . . he has a baby with him."

"What? A man wants to bring a baby in here?"

"I guess so."

"Why?"

"He says he found it," Cardwell said with a shrug. "He needs someplace to leave it while he finds out where it belongs. Or maybe he thinks it belongs to one of the girls."

Lily frowned. "None of my girls has been pregnant."

"Okay," Cardwell said, "I'll tell him."

"No, wait," Lily said. "He asked for me by name?"

"Nope."

"Then what?"

"He asked for the lady of the house."

"The lady of the house?"

"Yeah."

She pushed her chair back and got up.

"Leave him to me."

When the door opened, Clint saw a handsome woman in her forties, with long dark hair and pale skin.

"Jesus Christ," she said, looking at the boy. She also sniffed the air. "He stinks."

"I know," Clint said, "and I don't have any more shirts to use as diapers."

"Bring him inside, for Chrissake," she said, backing away from the door.

"Thank you."

Clint entered and at that moment three girls came out of the main sitting room, where they greeted their customers.

"Oh, a baby," one of them cooed.

"He's so cute," another said.

"And dirty," the third said.

"Girls," Lily said, "go and find me something to clean him with, and to put him in after he's clean."

"Towels!" one girl said.

"Pillowcases!" another said.

"And water," Lily said. "Bring them to my room." She looked at Clint. "You follow me."

"Yes, ma'am," Clint said, and followed her down a hallway to a room at the back of the house.

FOUR

Clint gave the baby up to the women and watched. If he'd had any doubts about a group of whores caring for a baby, they were quickly dispelled.

Lily took control. The other girls brought water and cloth. Lily washed the baby, who seemed to enjoy the attention. He cooed and laughed as she bathed him, and then she fashioned a diaper from a towel. Next she swathed him in a white sheet, which she cut to fit around him better. She also cut a hole in it, and dropped it over his head, and then sat him up. As she dried his hair, all the girls gathered around him, laughing.

"What's his name?" one of them asked, looking at Clint.

"I don't know."

"You haven't named him?" another girl asked.

"He's not mine to name," he said. "I found him."

"Where?" Lily asked. "Exactly."

"Just out there," he said, "about three miles outside of town. Just walking . . ."

"Barefoot?" one girl asked.

"Yes."

"Oh, his poor feet." They crowded around to examine the baby's feet, and then one of them offered to make some booties to protect them.

"Never mind," Lily said. "We'll go shopping and get him some things."

"Ooh, shopping!" one girl cried, and they all became excited.

"Not all of you!" Lily said. "In fact, I want you all to go back to work except . . . Angie and Helen."

The girls pouted and complained, but eventually they all left the room, leaving behind a tall blond girl named Angie, and a small brunette named Helen.

"You girls go and get dressed," Lily said. "I'll stay with the baby while you go and shop."

The girls clapped their hands excitedly.

"You'll shop for the baby!" Lily said quickly. "Not for yourselves. Understand?"

"Yes, ma'am."

"Get dressed," she said, "and then come back for money."

They turned and ran from the room.

"I'll pay for whatever they buy," Clint said.

Lily turned to look at him.

"I figured you would," she said.

"Will you keep the child here while I try to find out where he belongs?"

"I will," Lily said, "but you'd better hurry. If you take too long, these girls will not want to let the kid go."

"You'd raise him in a whorehouse?"

"Why not?" she asked. "Whores are the most honest people I know."

"I never thought of it that way," Clint said, "but I guess you're right."

"I never met a whore who didn't admit exactly what she was," Lily said.

"Unless she was paid to," Clint pointed out.

"Well . . . there's always that."

Lily picked the boy up and held him in her arms. Clint noticed as the woman pressed her nose to the boy's head and inhaled.

"Has he said anything?" she asked. "He looks about the age where he should have some words."

"He said, 'Mama.'"

"Mama," the boy said as if to prove he could.

"Well, then," Lily said, "that means he has a mama."

"That's what I thought," Clint said.

"Well," she said, walking back and forth and patting the boy on the back, "I don't know of anyone in town who's missing a baby. And I doubt this little boy walked three miles in his bare feet."

"I didn't see any wagons or ranches," Clint said.

"You must have come to town from the west."

"Yes."

"There are only a few ranches out that way," she said. "Most of them are north and east of town."

"I see."

"If you ride back out, then ride in circles, you're bound to come to a ranch," she told him. "There's the Reynolds place, and the Rocking C . . ."

"Any babies out there?"

"Not that I know of. But they might have visitors."

"Well, that sounds like good advice."

Lily studied Clint critically for a moment, then said, "Maybe you should get yourself something to eat first, though. He'll be all right here for a while."

"Another good idea," Clint said. "I'll also need to get a hotel room, and give my horse some rest."

"Go and do all that," Lily said. "I'll have the girls get the baby something to eat and drink as well as something to wear."

"All right," Clint said. He took some money out of his pocket and handed it to Lily. "Will that be enough?"

She smiled and said, "We'll make it enough."

"Overnight, all right?" Clint asked. "It'll be dark soon and—"

"Overnight's fine," Lily said. "I'll make up a bed for him."

"I can't thank you enough—"

"For taking him off your hands?"

"For helping the little guy," he said.

"Well," she said, "we're both doing that, aren't we?"

The girls came back in at that point. They were wearing modest cotton dresses and had scrubbed all the paint from their faces. They hovered around the baby, and accepted the money from Lily. As Clint left, she was giving them instructions as to what to buy.

FIVE

He reined in Eclipse in front of the first saloon he came to, a small place obviously owned by a man with no imagination, as the saloon was called No. 8. It reminded him of Deadwood, Saloon No. 5, where his friend Wild Bill Hickok had been killed.

He entered the saloon, which was almost empty. It was true to its exterior, small on the inside with only a few tables and a short, somewhat makeshift bar. It suited his purpose, though. He just needed a beer to wash away the trail dust before he saw to Eclipse's comfort, and his own.

"Beer," he told the bartender.

"Comin' up."

The fortyish barman drew him the beer and set the mug in front of him.

"Just get to town?" he asked.

"Rode in this minute," Clint said. He drank down half the beer. It wasn't ice cold, but it cut the dust. "Looks like you've got an election coming up."

"We do," the man said. "Mayoral election."

"Ah," Clint said. "Today wouldn't be election day, would it?"

"No, sir," the bartender said. "That's still two weeks away."

"Who's this fellow Lennon? Seems he has a lot of signs around town."

"That'd be Mayor Lennon."

"The incumbent?"

"That's right."

Clint sipped some more beer.

"Seems like his opponent isn't advertising himself as well as the mayor."

"That's because there ain't no opponent," the man said.

"What?"

"His honor runs unopposed every time," the bartender said.

"Every time?"

The man nodded.

"Been mayor goin' on twenty years."

"And nobody ever runs against him?"

"Nope."

"Why is that?"

The bartender hesitated, then shrugged and said, "Guess nobody else wants the job."

Clint had recently spent some time in Abilene, and the town had a similar situation, a mayor that nobody would ever run against. That situation had changed while he was there, due in large part to some actions by him. However, he had no intention of getting involved in the politics of any other towns he visited.

"Guess it must be a pretty thankless job," he said.

The bartender laughed shortly and said, "I wouldn't want it."

Clint finished his beer.

"Another one?"

"No, that'll do it for now," he said. "I've got to get my horse taken care of, and get myself a hotel room. Any suggestions?"

"Down the street, the Belle Flower Hotel. It's got pretty good rooms, and comfortable beds."

"Thanks." Clint dropped some money on the bar, sure that it was more than the beer was worth. The bartender didn't complain.

He got Eclipse situated in a livery stable where, as usual, the big Darley Arabian drew the admiration of the owner.

"Never seen an animal this magnificent before," the man said, running his hand over Eclipse's flanks. The big Darley had a sixth sense about people, could tell when somebody had good horse sense and knew what he was doing. If the animal trusted the man enough to let him touch him, then Clint felt content to leave the horse in the man's care.

Next he went to the Belle Flower Hotel. Like the saloon, it was small, but unlike the saloon, it was clean. The lobby was deserted as he entered, carrying his rifle and saddlebags. The desk clerk looked up and smiled, but didn't say a word until Clint had reached the desk.

"Can I help you, sir?"

"I need a room."

"Certainly. For how long?"

"I'm not sure," Clint said. "One or two nights."

The man turned the register so Clint could sign in.

"Are you here on business?" he asked.

"No," Clint answered, "I'm just . . . looking for some people."

"Ah, well, Mr. . . ." The clerk peered at the name, then stared at Clint with wide eyes. "Adams?"

"That's right."

The man reached behind him for a key, missed twice as he groped for one, then finally turned his head and grabbed one.

"Room five, sir," he said. "Uh, b-best in the house. Overlooks the street."

"Is there a balcony? Anything outside the window? A low roof?" Clint asked.

"No, sir, nothin' like that."

Clint snatched the key from the man's hand and said, "It'll be fine, then."

The room was large, well furnished—probably was, indeed, the best room in the house. Clint figured the nervous clerk was probably only going to charge him for a regular room. Unless his boss found out about it.

He walked to the window and looked out. He'd been lucky the women at the whorehouse wanted a baby around. It would give him time to get some food, and some rest, and then ride out in the morning and find out where the baby had come from.

He left his saddlebags and rifle in the room and went out to find a steak.

SIX

Just two blocks from the hotel, Clint found a small café. He actually smelled it before he got to it, and followed his nose. Inside, he secured a table away from the windows and ordered a steak dinner.

He was working his way through the overdone steak when Sheriff Murphy came walking in. Some of the other diners looked up at him as he went by them to Clint's table.

"Sheriff," Clint said. "Have a seat."

The man seemed to have cleaned up. When he sat and removed his hat, Clint saw that he'd combed his hair. And he was wearing cleaner clothes.

"If you were lookin' for a good steak, I could have told you where to go," he said.

"Good," Clint said, "tell me so I can get one for my next meal."

"I can tell you a couple of places," Murphy said.

"How about some coffee?" Clint asked.

"Sure."

Clint poured him a cup, and went back to work on the steak with his knife.

"The baby?" Murphy asked.

"I left him with Lily."

"Lily with a baby," Murphy said, shaking his head.

"You sent me there," Clint said. "All the girls will be taking care of him."

"Well, good for the boy," Murphy said. "I know a lot of men who'd like to be in that kid's place."

Clint laughed.

"How did you find me?"

"I stopped at the hotel," Murphy said. "The clerk told me you'd just left. He saw you turn this way. His name's Walter, by the way. You've made him very nervous."

"I hardly spoke to him."

"Well, once he saw your name . . . you must go through that a lot."

"Some."

"I hope he gave you a good room."

"Best in the house, he said."

"Good. What are your plans?"

"Tomorrow morning I'm going to ride out and see if I can find where the kid came from," Clint said. "He can't have walked very far."

"You didn't find anything on the way in, though."

"I probably just rode in the wrong direction. Lily told me about a Reynolds place, and a Rocking C?"

"Neither one of them would have a child that young around," Murphy said.

"Where would you suggest I go?"

"Beats me," Murphy said. "I can't think of anyplace that would have a baby . . ."

"What about the doctor?"

"He's too old to have a baby."

"I mean, maybe he'd know."

"Oh, well, yeah, that makes sense. That'd be Doc Simon. I can introduce you."

"Why don't we do that now?"

"Don't you want to finish your steak?"

"Actually," Clint said, putting the knife and fork down, "no. And do I dare have pie here?"

"No," Murphy said. "I'll take you to the doc, and then I'll show you where to get good pie."

"Sounds like a deal."

Clint grudgingly paid his bill, and they left.

The sheriff led the way several blocks to the doctor's office. The shingle outside said, DR. SIMON, G.P. The sheriff entered without knocking.

"Doc!" he shouted.

"Maybe he's with a patient," Clint said. "Maybe we shouldn't disturb—"

"It's after hours," Murphy said. "Ol' Doc don't work after office hours unless it's a real emergency."

A door opened and a man stepped in from another room.

"Murphy, what the hell are you bellowin' about?" the man asked.

He was tall, but slightly stooped, looked to be in his seventies.

"Doc, there here's Clint Adams."

Simon gave Clint an appraising look.

"You don't look shot."

"I'm not."

"Then what does the Gunsmith need with a sawbones?"

"He found a baby," Murphy said.

"What?"

"A baby," Clint said. "A little boy. I found him wandering around out in the middle of nowhere."

"Well, where is he?"

Clint hesitated.

"He took him to Maddy's," Murphy said.

The doctor's bushy white eyebrows went up.

"You find a toddler wandering around in the middle of nowhere," he said, "and you bring him to town and give him to a bunch of whores instead of bringin' him to the doctor?"

"I thought—"

"It was my idea, Doc," Murphy said. "I thought them gals might know something."

"Like how to take care of a baby?" Simon asked. "They're a bunch of whores, Tom."

"They're women," Clint said, "and they're taking good care of him."

"Okay," Doc Simon said, "then what do you want with me?"

"I was wondering if you know of anybody who was missing a baby," Clint said.

"A toddler, right?" Simon asked.

"I . . . I guess," Clint said.

"Well, he was walking, right?"

"Stumbling, was more like it."

"Then he's a toddler," Simon said. "I don't know of anybody who's missing a toddler."

"Do you know anybody who lives west of town who has a little boy?" Clint asked.

"West of town . . . no," Simons said. "The Wellmans, over at the Bar-W, they got some kids, but they're east of town and they don't have any kids under five."

"Well," Murphy said to Clint, "it was worth a try."

"I'll just have to ride out tomorrow and see what I can find," Clint said. "Thanks, Doc."

"If I was you," Simon said, "I'd bring that kid to see me so I can examine him."

"I'll do that, Doc," Clint said. "I should have thought of that myself."

"Yeah," Doc Simon said, "you should've. And come during office hours."

"I'll make sure I do," Clint said.

He and Sheriff Murphy left the office.

"Pleasant man," Clint said, outside.

"Lousy bedside manner," Murphy said, "but he's a helluva doctor."

"I guess that's what counts," Clint said.

SEVEN

Clint woke the next morning, armed with Tom Murphy's suggestions about where to eat. When Clint told him his breakfast of choice was steak and eggs, Murphy directed him to a café about three blocks from the hotel. If Clint had come out of the hotel the night before and turned left instead of right, he might have found it on his own.

He settled into a table among many of the townspeople, still managing to stay away from the windows. There were men sitting alone, and in pairs, couples with and without children. He saw no women sitting alone, or together with other women.

He attracted attention as he entered, but when he was seated, people went back to their own conversations. While he listened, he heard many of them talking about the upcoming election.

From what he could hear, not many of the diners were in favor of the current mayor repeating his term, but it also seemed that no one was willing to vote against him—if, indeed, anyone even ran against him.

When Clint's breakfast came, he decided to stop listening to conversations at the other tables and pay attention to his steak, which appeared to be cooked perfectly.

It was not only the steak, but the eggs and biscuits were also cooked to perfection. Clint thought that if the place Murphy suggested for dinner was as good as this, he was in for a treat.

After breakfast he walked to the livery stable where he had left Eclipse the night before.

"You takin' him out already?" the hostler said, disappointed.

"Just for a while," Clint said. "I'll be bringing him back later today."

"Oh, okay," the old man said. "I ain't never had an animal like this in my place before. I don't wanna give him up so soon."

"I understand."

"Want me to saddle 'im for you?"

"I'll saddle him myself," Clint said. "If you try, you might lose a finger."

The man showed Clint his left hand, which was missing a finger and a half, and said, "Wouldn't be the first time."

"I'll do it anyway," Clint said.

"Okay, mister," the hostler said, "as long as ya bring him back."

"I promise."

Clint mounted up and rode out of town, back the way he had ridden in.

He spent the better part of the afternoon riding in circles, stopping at houses and ranches, asking if anyone was missing a child. He couldn't imagine anyone would deny it, so he believed all the *no*'s he was getting. Apparently, no one in the area was missing a little boy.

He was just about ready to return to town—his stomach was growling loud enough to spook Eclipse—when he saw something in the distance. It wasn't a house, but something that looked like it was sticking up from the ground. It was over a rise, and when he topped it, he saw that it wasn't in the ground, just strewn about. It looked like a wagon—a buckboard, not a Conestoga—but it was in pieces, lying on its side. There were no horses anywhere. They had either been run off, or had simply gone off on their own.

He rode up to the wreckage, rode around it for a few moments before dismounting. There were personal belongings spread out around it, clothing, a couple of pieces of furniture, open and emptied suitcases.

Walking around, he didn't see any bodies, but he knew they'd be there. He could see the drag marks. He followed them to a pile of dirt, a hastily put together grave. He dug into it just enough to find a man's hand and a woman's foot. Two bodies, maybe more.

He went back to the wagon, looked around at the remnants of the dead people's lives with a new eye. He saw what he was looking for.

Baby clothes.

This was where the baby had come from.

No doubt the parents were in the grave. Whoever had killed them had simply left the baby alone, and he had wandered away, to be found by Clint.

Now he had to get back to town and come back with the sheriff, and transportation for the dead parents.

The child was now an orphan.

EIGHT

Clint entered the sheriff's office. The man looked up from his desk.

"You look like you've been riding awhile."

"All day."

"Find anything?"

Clint nodded. "I'm afraid I did," he said. "Two bodies—maybe more—in a hastily dug grave."

"Damn it!" Murphy said. "The kid's parents?"

"Looks like it," Clint said. "Their wagon was ransacked, and there's kid's clothes around."

"All right." The sheriff stood up. "I'll get some men and a buckboard, and then you can show us where they are."

"All right."

"If we hurry," the lawman said, grabbing his gun belt, "we can get back before dark."

"It's not far," Clint said. "Maybe a couple of miles. I'm figuring the kid walked about a mile."

"That's a pretty long way for a kid to walk barefoot," Murphy said as they left the office.

"That's what I was thinking," Clint said. "Pretty special kid."

* * *

While the sheriff was gathering his men and picking up a buckboard, Clint went to Maddy's to tell Lily what was happening.

A red-haired girl showed Clint into Lily's office. She was sitting behind her desk, holding the baby, who seemed clean, well diapered, and very happy.

"Well," she said, "I was starting to think you left town."

"I did," he said, "this morning."

"But you came back."

"I did."

He walked to the desk, reached out, and allowed the baby to grasp the index finger of his left hand. The boy had a good grip.

"What did you find?" she asked.

He didn't answer.

"You found the parents?"

"Yes."

"Dead."

He nodded.

"Are you sure it's them?"

"No," he said. "But I found a man and a woman dead, and their belongings were scattered about, including baby clothes."

She leaned forward and kissed the child on the head.

"Poor boy," she said.

"Can he stay here a little longer?" Clint asked. "I have to ride out with the sheriff to recover the bodies."

"He can stay as long as he has to," she said. "There's always one of the girls available to look after him."

"I'll probably come back tomorrow to take him to see the doctor," he told her.

"He seems fine," she said, "but that's probably a good idea."

He stroked the boy's hair, then said, "I guess I'd better go, Lily."

He started for the door, then turned back.

"I thought he had darker hair," he said.

"It was the dirt," she told him. "Now that it's washed, you can see that he's blond."

"Yes."

"Let me know what happens," she said.

"I will."

He met the sheriff, and two men with a buckboard, in front of the lawman's office.

"How's the kid?" Murphy asked.

"Seems okay," Clint said.

"I'd be okay, too, if I had a buncha whores lookin' after me," the first man said, laughing.

"The boy's parents may be dead," Clint said. "Slaughtered. You find that funny, too?"

"No, sir," the man said.

"Then shut up," Murphy said. "Don't even talk during the ride out there."

The man sulked.

"Okay," Murphy said to Clint, "you might as well take the lead."

"Right."

Clint led them directly to the sight of the burial. The two men jumped down from the buckboard, retrieved shovels from the back, and began to dig.

"When you get them dug up, lay them out on the bed of the buckboard," Murphy told them.

"What are you gonna do, Sheriff?" the second man asked.

"Mr. Adams and me are gonna have a look around, see what we can recover of their belongings. Something's got to tell us who they are."

Clint and Murphy walked back to the overturned buckboard and started there. They picked up pieces of the dead people's lives, set them on the back of the other buckboard. Eventually, there were three bodies in that buckboard with all the belongings.

"Another child," Murphy said, shaking his head. "Looks like a teenage girl, maybe younger. Twelve?"

"Probably," Clint said.

Clint leaned over to examine the bodies.

"All shot."

"Why leave the boy?" Murphy wondered. "Why kill the parents and the sister, and leave the boy?"

"Because he can't say what he saw," Clint said. "He can't talk. Besides, they probably thought he'd die out here. Either an animal would get him because he was helpless, or he'd just . . . die."

"That's it," the men said, returning to the buckboard with the shovels. "No more bodies."

"All right," Murphy said. "Wait for us on the buckboard."

They nodded, put the shovels on the bed with the bodies and property, and climbed up onto the seat.

"I'm going to take another walk around, look at the ground."

"Tracks?"

"Yes. Might give us some idea of how many killers there were," Clint said.

"I'll wait here," Murphy said. "I'm no tracker, and I've already trampled all over the tracks."

"I'll only be a few minutes."

Murphy nodded.

Clint walked around, picked out the tracks of the horses he thought had been ridden, and hadn't been made by the team. Then he returned to the buckboard.

"How many?"

"Half a dozen, maybe more," Clint said.

"Bastards! Any identifying marks?"

"One set of tracks looks like it has a chip on the left

forefoot," Clint said. "Should help us identify tracks, if they don't change the shoe."

"Well," Murphy said, "I guess we got what we came for. It's gettin' dark. Let's head back."

Clint nodded, and they mounted up.

NINE

It was dark when they reached town. Murphy had to bother Doc Simon again after business hours, as well as the undertaker.

"Take them to Albert's," the doctor said, using the undertaker's first name. "I'll examine them there."

"Right," Murphy said.

All four men piled back into the buckboard and went to the undertaker's. The two hired hands carried the bodies inside.

"What about the property?" the first man, Evans, asked.

"Take it over to my office," Murphy said, jumping off the wagon. "All of it. We'll look it over there."

He and the other man, Vincent, got back on the buckboard and drove it over to the sheriff's office.

Inside, the undertaker, Albert Frost, was looking at the bodies, laid out on three tables in his back room.

"What do you want me to do, Sheriff?" he asked.

"We're waiting for Doc Simon, Albert," Murphy said. "We'll let him have a look first, then we'll decide what you're gonna do. Okay?"

"Okay with me, Sheriff," Frost said.

At that moment the doctor entered, carrying his black bag.

"All right," he said, "everybody out."

"How long, Doc?" Murphy asked.

"I don't know, Sheriff," Simon said. "Don't you have something else to do?"

"Yeah," Murphy said, "actually we do." He looked at Clint. "Want to go look at their belongings?"

"Yeah, thanks."

"And we can get something to eat," the sheriff said as they left. "I'll take you to that place I told you about . . ."

They decided to eat first, so Murphy led the way to the restaurant he promised Clint had the best steak in town. There was no name over the door, but Murphy said everybody called it Kate's.

"Is the Kate the owner?"

"No."

"The cook?"

"No."

"Then why's it called Kate's?"

"Nobody knows."

They got a table in the back. Clint assumed it was Murphy's regular table, as the other diners greeted him as they walked across the floor.

After they were seated, Clint said, "That reminds me of something else."

"What's that?"

"If the whorehouse is run by Lily, why did you call it Maddy's?"

"Force of habit," Murphy said. "Used to be run by a woman named Madelyn. Lily was one of her girls. When Maddy died, she left it to Lily."

"Well," Clint said, "at least that makes sense."

They each ordered a steak dinner, and Clint realized the sheriff was right. The steak was excellent, probably the best in town. Not the best he'd ever had, but very good.

They indulged in small talk while they ate, nothing important until Clint asked about the election.

"What about it?"

"Why bother if nobody's running against the incumbent?"

"The mayor insists on it," the sheriff said. "He says it's got to be a fair and honest election."

"And is it?"

"Why do you care?"

"I don't," Clint said. "I'm just making conversation."

"Well, don't," the sheriff said, looking around. "It ain't healthy."

"Okay, Sheriff," Clint said. "Whatever you say."

They finished their dinner in silence, didn't have dessert, and left to go to Murphy's office.

"Sorry about that," Murphy said on the way. "It just ain't healthy to talk about the mayor in public."

"So it's not a fair and honest election?"

"Mr. Adams," Sheriff Murphy said, "there ain't nothing fair and honest about our esteemed mayor."

They walked in silence a little longer, and then Clint said, "Call me Clint."

TEN

When they reached the office, the two men and the buckboard were gone, but the belongings of the dead people were strewn about the sheriff's office.

"Idiots," Murphy said. "They should have piled up everything in one of the cells."

"I guess you should've told them."

"We can move it in there ourselves," Clint said, "as we look it over."

"Yeah, sure. Let's get started."

They went through the dead parents' clothes and some of their smaller belongings such as a shaving kit, a sewing basket, and several small suitcases into which they had stuffed discarded clothes. There was some larger furniture still out at the site—a dresser, a chest of drawers, a cedar chest, all of which had been emptied by the killers.

"Notice what's missing?" Clint asked as they came out of the cell block, where they had piled everything into one cell.

"A wallet," the sheriff said, "or anything saying who they were."

"No letters either," Clint said. "A family like this, the mother would most likely save all her letters."

"So the killers were smart enough to take them," Murphy said, "not wanting these people to be identified."

"I think one thing's pretty certain, though," Clint said.

"And what's that?"

"They were the boy's family," Clint said. "There are enough boy's clothes to indicate that. By the way, can I take them over to Lily's?"

"Sure," Murphy said, "use one of the small suitcases."

Clint went back into the cell block, came out a few minutes later with a small suitcase filled with boy's clothes, and some toys.

Murphy was seated behind his desk, his hat and gun belt hanging on the wall. He looked tired, his hair—or what was left of it—lank and thin. In fact, he looked more like the swamper Clint had thought he was when he first saw him.

"Coffee?" Clint asked.

"Should be ready," Murphy said. He had put a pot on the stove when they got there.

Clint went to it and poured two mugs full. It was very black and strong. He carried one to the desk, set it down in front of Murphy, and then sat across from him.

"What will you do now?" Murphy asked.

"Tomorrow I'll take the boy to the doc's so he can look him over,"

"That ain't gonna help find out who he is," Murphy said. "Or get us to any of his relatives."

"I could go out to the site again, look around. Maybe the killers left something behind. Might be an envelope or letter blowing around out there."

"That's a long shot."

"I'm a gambler."

The office door opened and Doc Simon walked in with his bag.

"Finished?" the lawman asked.

"I'm here, ain't I?" Simon asked. "Any more of that coffee?"

"I'll get you a cup," Clint said, standing. "Have a seat."

The doctor took his chair, accepted a mug of coffee. Clint remained standing.

"What'd you find, Doc?" Murphy said.

"They're all dead," Simons said, and sipped the coffee.

"Is that supposed to be funny?" Clint asked.

Simon looked up at him.

"Am I smiling?" he asked.

"Sorry."

"They were all shot, the man three times, the woman twice, and the little girl once."

"Bastards!" Murphy said.

"And both women—the woman and the girl, that is— were raped."

"The girl, too?" Clint asked.

Simon nodded.

"How old was she, do you think?"

"She was big for her age," the doctor said. "Eleven or twelve."

"Bastards," Murphy said again.

"How long?" Clint asked.

"Were they buried?"

Clint nodded.

"Just yesterday," Simon said. "Probably within hours of you finding the boy. They are his folks, aren't they?"

"Looks like it," Clint said.

"Did you find anything that would identify them?" Simon asked. "Tell you where they're from?"

"Nothing."

"So you can't find any of the boy's family?"

"Not so far."

Simon finished his coffee, set the cup down on the desk, and stood up.

"Are you still bringing him to me so I can examine him?" he asked.

"Tomorrow morning."

"Try to make it during business hours, okay?"

"I'll do that, Doc."

Simon nodded, said, "Sheriff," and left.

"He's a hard man," Clint said.

"Seeing some of the things he sees," Sheriff Murphy said, "I guess that's a good thing."

"I'm going to go through their things once more before I go back to my hotel. Is that okay with you?"

"Be my guest," Murphy said.

Clint poured another cup of coffee to take into the cell block with him.

ELEVEN

Clint couldn't find anything his second time through the dead family's things, so he went back to his hotel room for the night. He made a conscious decision not to spend any time that night in a saloon, either nursing a couple of beers or playing some poker. He wanted to get an early start in the morning.

Which he did. He rose early, had breakfast the same place as the day before, and then went to Maddy's to pick up the boy. He brought the bag of clothes with him.

"I thought we might change him into something of his own before I took him to the doctor," he said to Lily after he was let in.

"Great," she said, putting her hand out. "Let me find something for him."

"Where is he?"

"Upstairs with two of the girls," she said. "They're playing with him. I'll go up and dress him. You wait here in my office."

"Okay."

She took the bag with her and left. He was curious about her, almost enough to snoop around her office, but just as he was making up his mind, the door opened and a girl walked in. He recognized her as the blonde Lily had sent to do the shopping for the boy.

"Angie, right?" he asked.

"You remembered," she said. "I'm flattered." She was wearing a filmy robe that showed all her curves, and some shadowed cleavage beneath it. "Lily sent me down to keep you company while she dresses our boy."

"Your boy?" he asked.

She shrugged. "That's how we girls have been thinkin' about him."

"I see."

"We heard you found his family dead," she said. "I guess we'll never know his name, then. We should probably give him one."

"You can all work on it while I take him to the doctor's," Clint said.

"Oh, he's fine," she said. "And he's so happy."

"That's good."

"In fact," she said, "maybe we should call him Happy."

"That would make him sound like a clown."

She laughed and said, "You're right. And what about you?"

"What about me?"

"What do we call you?"

"Clint," he said, "just call me Clint."

"So this is our formal introduction," she said, sticking out her hand. "Hi, Clint, I'm Angie."

"Hi, Angie," he said, shaking her hand.

She held on to his hand longer than necessary, moistened her lips with the tip of her tongue. He didn't know what else might have happened if Lily hadn't walked in at that point, carrying the boy.

"Down, Angie!" she said. "He's not here for our particular brand of business."

"Too bad," Angie said. She turned, headed for the door, saying over her shoulder, "See you later, Clint."

As she left the room, Lily approached Clint and held the baby out to him.

"You're not one of the ones who wants to name him Happy, are you?"

"What?"

"Just something Angie said."

"Happy? Well," she said, stroking the baby's face, "he is kind of happy. But wouldn't that make him sound like a clown?"

"Just what I said," Clint commented. "Okay, I'll bring the boy back after the doc sees him."

"Fine," she said. "I guess he can stay here until the law decides what to do with him."

Clint nodded his thanks and left with the boy.

Hiram Anderson reined his horse in by the copse of trees and waited. He was five minutes early for his meeting with Milton Perryman. In a matter of seconds, though, he heard the horses approaching. Perryman and two of his men topped the rise and appeared. His horse fidgeted impatiently as they rode up to him.

"Anderson," Perryman said.

"Mr. Perryman."

"Tell me," the rancher said, "are you under the impression that your job is done?"

"What? Well, yes, sir. I mean . . . they're dead. We buried 'em and all."

"Not all of them."

"Well, no . . . I mean . . . not the kid . . . but . . . he was out there all alone . . ."

"So you couldn't kill the child, but you could leave him out there to die?"

"Yes, sir," Hiram said. "I mean, no, sir."

"When I give a man a job, I expect him to do it," Perryman said. "All of it."

"I'm sorry, Mr. Perryman," Hiram said, "but me and Willie, we just couldn't shoot that little boy."

"But I'll bet you raped the woman."

"Well, yeah . . ."

"And the little girl?"

"She wasn't so little," Hiram said. "Twelve, or so. Plenty old enough for Willie."

Perryman shook his head.

"I won't be needing you anymore, Anderson," he said.

"But . . . we still get paid for what we did, right?" Hiram asked. "I mean, Willie's waitin' for me to come with the money."

"I see," Perryman said. "Yes, you'll get paid." He turned his horse, started away, and said to his men, "Pay him."

"Two hundred . . . hey—" Hiram said as the two men drew their guns.

TWELVE

"How is he?" Clint asked.

The boy was seated on the doctor's examining table, playing with Simon's stethoscope as it hung around the doctor's neck.

The doctor finished probing the boy's chest and belly, turned his head to Clint.

"He's a little undernourished, but generally in good health," he said. "His parents must not have been able to feed him well. He wasn't wandering out there long enough to become undernourished."

"No, he wasn't."

The doctor put the boy's shirt back on, patted him on the cheek, and took his stethoscope away from him. The boy looked as if he might cry, but he didn't.

"What are you going to do with him?" Simon asked.

"For now, leave him at Maddy's," Clint said. "The girls there like him; they'll take good care of him."

"Make sure they feed him," the doctor said.

"Oh, they're feeding him just fine, but what do you suggest I do with him in the long run?" Clint asked.

"Well, there are a couple of families around here who'd like a baby."

"That doesn't sound like a bad idea," Clint said. "Let a family adopt him."

"Just let me know," Simon said. "I can talk to them, see which one would be a better fit. Or which one wants him more."

Clint picked the child up. The boy's arms immediately went around his neck. He was surprised how good they felt there.

"You're talking about giving him to them, right?"

"Of course," the doctor said. "You're not thinking that I'd sell him, are you?"

"No," Clint said, "of course not. What do I owe you?"

"Nothing," Simon said. "Don't worry about it."

"Thanks, Doc."

Clint turned and left the office.

Milton Perryman dismounted, let one of his ranch hands take his horse. He mounted the steps of his house and went inside.

"Well?" his wife asked.

"They killed the parents, and the girl," he said.

"What about the boy?"

"No."

She looked at Perryman with a knitted brow that did nothing to hide her beauty. She was ten years younger than him, but at forty she felt like an old lady. No amount of praise about how beautiful she was could help.

"Then where is he?"

"They just . . . let him go."

"You mean he's wandering around alone out there?"

"I suppose so," Perryman said.

"He won't last long," she said. "He'll die, Milton, of hunger or . . . or worse. Some animal will get him."

Perryman studied her.

"Are you upset they didn't kill him? Or that he's out there all alone?"

"Both," she said. "I would rather they finished it than leave him out there."

"The men will be going to town to see if there's any news," Perryman said.

"What about the men who did it?"

"One's dead," he said, "the other one is as good as."

"You better find him."

"We will."

She was wearing a simple high-necked cotton dress, had her arms crossed, cradling herself. No one seeing her would guess she was married to the richest man in the county.

"Are you hungry?" she asked.

"Actually, I am."

"I'll fix you something."

"Thanks, Veronica."

She nodded and went to the kitchen. Although she had servants in the house, she sometimes liked to do the cooking and cleaning herself.

He walked to a sideboard in the living room and poured himself a drink. He drank it thoughtfully, pondering the fate of that little boy.

Lily took the boy from Clint, having to pry his arms from around his neck.

"He likes you," she said.

"Yeah, well, I like him, too."

She turned and handed the baby to the little brunette, Helen.

"Take him to his room," she said.

"Yes, ma'am."

"And stay with him."

"I will."

The girl turned and left the room.

"He has his own room?" Clint asked.

"For now. What'd the doc say?"

"He's pretty healthy," Clint said, "just a little undernourished."

"We'll feed him good here."

"I know you will, Lily. I appreciate it. You should let me pay you."

"Why? He's not yours."

"He's my responsibility."

"Why?" she asked. "You could ride out right now and forget about him."

"I don't think I could do that, Lily," he said. "Not until I know he's all right."

She smiled.

"You're a good man, Clint Adams. I didn't expect that from a man like you."

"Like me?"

"The Gunsmith."

"Who told you?"

"It's around town."

"Great," Clint said. "That means sooner or later somebody's going to get itchy."

"Itchy?"

"To try me," Clint said. "Or shoot me in the back."

"That's the life you lead," she said. "The life you chose."

"It's the life I lead," he agreed. "But it's not the life I chose."

"Then you take him," she said.

"What?"

"Why don't you take the boy?" she said. "Change your life. Be a father."

"I'm nobody's father," Clint said. "I couldn't be."

"I've seen you with him, Clint," she said. "I think you're wrong."

"Well, that's not on this particular table," Clint said. "But I'll do my best to make sure he ends up someplace he'll be loved and cared for."

She smiled and said, "See? That's exactly what a father would say."

THIRTEEN

Sheriff Tom Murphy looked up as his office door opened and Willie Delvin walked in. Willie was an odd-job man in town, and would pretty much do anything for a nickel.

"What can I do for you, Willie?"

"Ya gotta hide me, Sheriff."

"Hide you?" Murphy asked. "Why? From who?"

"I can't tell ya."

"Can't tell me why? Or from who?"

"Either one," Willie said.

"Then why should I hide you?"

"I did a bad thing," Willie said.

"How bad?"

"Really bad." Willie, who was in his mid-twenties, was almost in tears and was very close to falling to his knees.

"Willie," Murphy said, "I can't help you unless you tell me what you did."

"I can't," Willie said, shaking his head, "I can't . . ."

"Then get out, Willie," Murphy said. "You're wasting my time."

"Sheriff—"

"Come back when you want to tell me the whole story," Murphy said.

Willie looked as if he was about to cry, but he turned and left the office.

"Goddamned idiot!" Murphy muttered.

Willie knew that Hiram Anderson was dead. If he weren't, he would have already been back with the money they were owed. Hiram had come to him with the job, which he said would be an easy one.

"Just some Easterners comin' out here to steal our land," he'd said.

"I ain't got no land."

"It don't matter," Hiram told him. "We'll be gettin' paid a lot of money. That's the only part that matters."

But the job hadn't gone so easy. They didn't know there'd be a baby boy on the wagon. The girl, that was okay. After all, she was about twelve. Plenty old enough for what Willie wanted. And the mother, she was tasty enough for Hiram. They'd made the husband watch, then made the women watch while they killed him. But after they killed the females, they saw the boy in the wagon.

"What do we do with him?" Willie asked.

"Shoot 'im," Hiram said.

"Okay, well . . . Wait. You mean me?"

"Yeah, you," Hiram sad. "Shoot him."

Willie had looked at the boy, at that point still sitting in the back of the buckboard.

"I ain't killin' no kid."

"You raped and killed the girl."

"She wasn't no kid," Willie said. "That's a . . . a baby. I ain't killin' no baby."

"So what do we do?" Hiram had asked. "We gotta collect our pay."

They stared at the boy in the buckboard, who stared back at them calmly, despite the fact that his family was lying on the ground, dead.

"I got it," Hiram had said.

"What?"

"We leave 'im."

"What?"

"Just leave 'im," Hiram said. "Let 'im go."

"Out here?"

"Why not?"

"He'll . . . he'll die," Willie said. "Some animal will get 'im, or he'll just . . . die."

"So?"

"What will you tell Mr. Perryman?"

"I'll tell him the job's done," Hiram had said. "And I'll bring back our money."

"Ya don't want me to go with you?"

"Naw," Hiram said, "I'll collect the money and meet you in town."

Now that Hiram wasn't back with the money, Willie knew it was bad news. If Mr. Perryman had found out that the boy was alive—and Willie had heard the talk in town—then he'd probably had Hiram killed.

Or . . . Hiram had gotten paid, and had left town with all the money.

Either way, Willie was nervous, and scared.

FOURTEEN

Clint was having a beer in the No. 8 saloon when Sheriff Murphy walked in.

"Have a beer?" Clint asked.

"You buyin'?"

"Naturally."

"Then yeah."

Clint waved to the bartender, who brought over two full mugs and set them down.

"What are you doin' here?" the sheriff asked after a sip. "I thought you'd be gettin' ready to leave town."

"Not just yet," Clint said.

"Then what's your plan?"

"The best thing for me to do," Clint said, "is find out who killed the boy's family."

"You got any ideas at this point?" Murphy said.

"There are two possibilities," Clint said. "They were killed randomly by outlaws, or they were killed for personal reasons."

"Personal . . . you think somebody knew who they were and had them killed?"

"I said it was one possibility," Clint reminded him, "but it's the one I'm going to pursue for now."

"And how will you start?"

"That track I told you about?" Clint said. "The horse with the chipped shoe?"

"You gonna look at all the shoes in town?"

"Not exactly," Clint said, "but I can start with the liveries here in town, see if anyone has had a shoe changed. Or if the track is visible around them. I find that horse, I find the killers."

Murphy suddenly acquired a brooding look on his face.

"What is it?" Clint asked.

"I think I may have made a mistake," he said. "Maybe because I'm impatient, or maybe because I don't suffer fools."

"What'd you do?"

"Fella named Willie Delvin came into my office a little while ago," Murphy said. "He's kinda an odd-job man in town, will do anything for money."

"Including murder?"

"Well, I wouldn't have thought so, but today he was telling me he done something terrible, and he wanted to talk to me about it."

"And?"

"He wanted to talk to me about it without tellin' me that it was."

"You couldn't get it out of him?"

"I didn't try," Murphy said. "That's what my mistake was. What if he was talking about killin' that family?"

"Well, can't we find him and ask him?"

"We can try," Murphy said. "The shape he was in, I'm sure he was either going to head for the nearest saloon, or go into hidin'."

"How long ago was this?"

"Not even an hour."

Clint put his beer down.

"What are we waiting for?"

"Like I said," Murphy replied, "I don't think Willie is up to murder, but—"

"It's a place to start," Clint said, heading for the door.

Murphy drank down half his beer, set the mug back on the bar, and followed.

There were three livery stables in town. Clint decided to leave the one he'd put Eclipse in for last.

But the first two liveries proved to be no help, so in the end he pinned his hopes on the third.

"You're not back to take him out again, are you?" the hostler asked. He looked at Murphy. "Sheriff."

"Andy." Clint hadn't known his name before that.

"Andy, we're looking for a horse," he said.

"What? Another horse? This one ain't good enough for you?"

"I'm looking for a man," Clint said. "If I find his horse, I find the man."

"Ah, I understand," Andy said. "What kind of horse?"

"One with a chipped shoe on its left forefoot."

"Oh, I see," Andy said. "We don't know the man or the horse, just the hoof."

"Exactly."

"Have you replaced such a shoe lately, Andy?" Murphy asked.

"No, Sheriff, I ain't."

"Have you seen one?" Clint asked.

"No."

"What about tracks?" Clint asked.

"You can look around at the tracks here," Andy said. "And you can look at the horses in the stalls, and in the corral out back."

Clint looked at Sheriff Murphy, who nodded. "I'll take the corral."

Clint nodded. He went from stall to stall, lifting the horses' legs and examining the shoes. He did not find the one that was chipped.

After that he and the sheriff walked about, examining

the ground for the chipped track. So many horses had gone through the livery, though, that it was difficult to tell one track from the other. But Clint was stubborn, and relentless, and finally he pointed and said, "Sheriff, here."

Sheriff Murphy rushed over. They were outside, by the corral.

"Is that it?" he asked.

Clint, who was crouched down on a single knee, pointed again and the sheriff leaned over.

"That's the one?"

Clint stood.

"Then where's the damn horse?" Murphy asked, straightening. "In the corral?"

"Maybe."

"I couldn't have missed it."

"Then it's not in the corral."

The sheriff seemed upset.

"Do you want to check for yourself?"

"No," Clint said, shaking his head. "If you didn't find it, then it's not there."

"Can you tell how fresh the track is?"

"It's overlayed by others," Clint told him, "so it's not very fresh."

"Can you follow it?"

"It's one hoofprint right now, Sheriff," Clint said. "I'll have to keep looking to see if I can pick up a trail."

"I'll help."

"You might as well go back to your work," Clint said. "If I find it, I'll let you know. Also, you can keep looking for your friend Willie."

"He's no friend of mine," Murphy said. "But I'll keep lookin', and see you later."

The sheriff went off to do his part, and Clint once again aimed his gaze downward.

FIFTEEN

Clint was not an expert tracker.

He was a good tracker, and didn't usually need help, but there were times when he needed to recruit an expert to help him. This might have been one of those times—except that he got lucky.

He walked about a hundred yards from the barn, studying the ground, and came upon a set of tracks that contained the chipped horseshoe. It looked like the rider of that horse was with at least one other rider.

He returned to the stable to saddle Eclipse.

Before leaving town, he rode back to the sheriff's office, found Murphy on the street out front.

"You look like you found something."

"I did," Clint said. "Tracks. Two horses, one of them with the chipped horseshoe."

"Let me saddle up—"

"No, I'll do it alone," Clint said. "You stay here and find Willie, if you can."

"I'm waitin' here for word from somebody who might know where he is."

"Good," Clint said. "Maybe one of us will find out something today."

Clint rode back the way he had come, circled the livery stable, then continued on a hundred yards or so to find the tracks again. From there he simply followed them . . .

. . . to the body.

The trail led him about a mile out of town, where the tracks split. He dismounted, studied the ground, made sure he was following the right set of tracks before remounting and starting off again. he could always come back to this point and pick up the other trail if he had to.

He kept his eyes down, following the tracks, but when he lifted his head, he saw the horse in the distance. Abandoning the tracks, he rode directly for the horse. As he approached, he slowed, so as not to spook the steeldust.

"Easy, fella," Clint said, dismounting slowly himself. Luckily, it seemed as if Eclipse was having a calming effect on the other animal. Clint reached him, patted his neck, and lifted his hoof. He had the chipped horseshoe.

"Well, okay," he said, stroking the animal's neck again, "you're the horse I was looking for. Now where's the rider?"

He wondered how far this horse had wandered. Looking around, there was nothing immediately in sight to help him.

"I guess I'll have to go back to the tracks," he said. "And you're coming with me."

He mounted Eclipse again, and keeping hold of the other horse's reins, he rode back to where he had left the trail. Finding it again, he resumed following it.

He rode for another half hour before he saw the tree on top of a hill. It was a good landmark, a fine place to meet someone, like somebody who was supposed to pay you. Clint had a feeling he knew what had happened, and when he reached the tree, he saw that he was right.

He dismounted, secured the steeldust's reins to his saddle, so that Eclipse would hold the animal steady.

He walked to the tree, leaned over the body that was lying beneath it. He'd been shot twice.

"You thought you were getting paid, didn't you, pal?" he asked the body.

He searched his pockets, didn't find anything—no money, no identification. Maybe there'd be something on the horse. He checked the saddlebags, and came up with a few items. Whoever had killed the man had stripped him of everything in his pockets—one pocket had been turned inside out—but maybe the horse had spooked when they shot the man, and run off and then returned.

He found a dirty shirt, some extra shells, an extra gun— an old Navy Colt—some dried beef jerky, a wad of tobacco, and a letter addressed to someone named Hiram Anderson.

"Hello, Mr. Anderson," he said to the body. "Let's go for a ride."

SIXTEEN

"That's Willie's partner," Sheriff Murphy said.

They were standing in front of his office, examining the body Clint had brought in slung over the saddle.

"Who is he?" Clint asked.

"His name's Hiram Anderson."

"What does he do?"

"The same as Willie," Murphy said, "anything he gets paid to do, but the difference is, I can see Hiram killing that family."

"And the rapes?"

"Oh, that I can see them both doin'," Murphy said. "I think Willie would stand by and watch Hiram do the killin', and then join in the fun."

"Fun," Clint said.

"Sorry," Murphy said. "I used the wrong word. I didn't mean—"

"That's okay," Clint said. "I know what you meant."

"Thanks," Murphy said. He examined the body further. "Looks like whoever he did the job for paid him off in a way he wasn't ready for."

"Maybe," Clint said, "they weren't happy with the way it came out."

"The boy, you mean?"

Clint nodded.

"His employer may have hired him to kill the whole family, and he didn't."

"Good point."

"Who has that much power and wealth around here?" Clint asked. "Who uses killers for hire?"

"Well," Murphy said, "that's hard to say. There are quite a few rich ranchers in the county."

"I want all their names and I'd like to know where to find them."

"What are you gonna do?" Murphy asked. "Ride up to them and ask them if they had a whole family killed?"

"You know," Clint said, "I might just do exactly that."

Clint left it to Murphy to take Anderson's body over to the undertaker's office. He rode back out to where the trail broke off into two, and started following the other one. Assuming that this trail was left by Willie Delvin, he hoped to find the man at the end of it. Wherever it led.

But he never got there.

He was following the tracks, eyes fixed on the ground, when he heard several horses approaching him. He lifted his eyed and saw five riders, reined Eclipse in to wait for them.

They didn't look like they were there to greet him.

"You're on Perryman land," one of them said when they'd reined in their horses in front of him.

"So?"

The speaker was older than the other four, so Clint assumed he was the leader, possibly the foreman. They were all cowboys, but they all wore guns.

"I didn't see any signs posted," he went on.

"Don't need any," the man said. "Everybody knows you don't ride across Perryman land."

"Really?" Clint asked. "Then how am I supposed to go from one point to another?"

The man grinned at him without humor and said, "You go around."

"Well now," Clint said, "that would just take entirely too long."

"That's too bad," the man said, "because you're gonna turn around right now and go back the way you came."

"What's your name?" Clint asked.

"Kane," the man said. "Harry Kane. I'm the foreman of the Perryman ranch."

"Well, Mr. Kane," Clint said, "I'm tracking somebody and the trail leads right through here. So if you and your men would move aside, I'll get back to it, and I'll be off Perryman land in no time at all."

"Mister," Kane said, "you ain't hearin' me. Turn around and go back the way you come."

"You're not hearing me, Kane," Clint said. "I said no."

"You're makin' this harder than it should be, friend," Kane said. "We don't wanna kill you just because you rode onto our land. So I'm gonna have my boys drag you off your horse and teach you a little lesson."

"That's not going to happen," Clint said with finality.

"Oh? And who's gonna stop them?"

"I am," Clint said. "I'll kill the first man who dismounts. I won't have hands laid on me."

"Then you don't leave us any choice but to shoot you out of your saddle," Kane said.

"Same difference," Clint said. "I'll kill the first man who touches his gun."

"You'll get one man," Kane said, "and the rest of us will get you."

"I'll get more than one, friend," Clint said, "but suppose I do only get one? Who wants to be that man?"

He watched as the ranch hands exchanged looks. They were hired to work as cowboys, not as gunmen.

"Look at your men, Mr. Kane," Clint said. "They're a little nervous."

Kane looked around. None of his men were able to look him in the eye.

"It don't matter," Kane said. "I'll kill you myself."

"You better think twice," Clint said.

"The thinkin's been done—" Kane started, but before he finished his statement, he went for his gun.

Clint drew cleanly and shot Kane right from his saddle. Then he holstered his gun.

"Who's next?" he asked.

The other men were stunned at the speed with which Clint had dispatched their foreman. None of them moved; they just stared at Clint, and at their dead boss.

"Pick him up and take him back to your ranch," Clint said. "Tell your boss you need a new ramrod."

Three of the men dismounted, picked up their fallen foreman, and tossed him over his saddle.

"And you better tell the story the way it happened," Clint told them. "That he gave me no choice."

The man who had not dismounted—now the oldest of the four remaining men—asked, "Mister . . . who are you?"

"My name's Clint Adams," Clint said. "Tell your boss if he wants to take this up with me, he can find me in Chester."

"C-Clint Adams?" the man asked, after swallowing. The other men all stopped what they were doing and stared at Clint, wide-eyed.

"That's right."

"Jesus, you're—"

"Yeah, yeah," Clint said. "I know who I am. Now take your foreman and get going."

The three men recovered from their shock and mounted their horses. One of then leaned down to grab the reins of the dead foreman's horse.

Clint watched the men ride off, waited until they were out of sight before he returned his gaze to the trail he was following.

SEVENTEEN

When the men got back to the Perryman ranch, they looked to the oldest one for orders, since the foreman was dead.

"Take him over to the barn with the horses," Jason Kendall said. "I'll see what the boss wants to do with him."

"Right."

Kendall handed his horse over, and walked to the house. When he knocked on the door, the housekeeper answered. She was a pretty girl who lived on one of the nearby farms.

"Hello, Katy."

"Mr. Kendall."

"Come on, Katy," he said. "I told you it's okay to call me Jason."

"That's okay, Mr. Kendall," she said. "I'd rather not."

"Is the boss in his office?"

"No, he's in the dining room. I don't think you should bother him."

"That's okay, Katy," he said. "I think he's gonna want to hear this."

"I can't—" she said, but he brushed past her and walked to the dining room.

Milton Perryman was sitting at a long dining room table,

a napkin tied around his neck, working on a full chicken on the plate in front of him.

"What the hell, Jason?" he said. "I'm eating."

"Kane's dead."

Perryman put his knife and fork down.

"What?"

"Dead," Kendall said. "Killed."

"By who?"

"Clint Adams," Kendall said. "The Gunsmith."

"What the hell was he doing going up against the Gunsmith?" Perryman asked. "And what the hell is that gunman doing around here?"

"I don't know," Kendall said, "but he was ridin' across your land and Kane wanted to stop him."

"Did Kane know who he was?"

"No."

"It probably wouldn't have made a difference," Perryman said. "Kane was an idiot."

"He was the foreman."

"I was going to replace him anyway," Perryman said. "With you."

"Me?"

"Do you want the job?"

"Well . . . yeah."

"Good," Perryman said, picking up his knife and fork again. "You'll ride into town with me tomorrow."

"And do what?"

"We'll see if we can get the Gunsmith arrested," Perryman said. "We can't just let him get away with killing one of our men—even an idiot like Kane." Perryman looked at Kendall. "I'd like to finish eating now."

"Yes, sir," Kendall said. "Uh, what do you want us to do with Kane's body?"

"Bury it," Perryman said, waving with his knife, "somewhere."

"Yes, sir." He turned and started walking toward the door.

"Oh, wait," Perryman called out, stopping Kendall in his tracks. "Send me Walt Billings in about half an hour."

"Yes, sir."

After being braced on Perryman land, Clint expected the trail to lead him there, but in the end it petered out near a stream. He didn't know if he was still on Perryman land or not, but he took his time, rode up and down the stream, in case the rider had used the stream to cover his tracks. However, he did not find the trail again, and had to assume that he had simply lost it.

It took him about a half hour of riding to realize how close he was to Chester again. The trail had taken him in a circle and led him back toward town.

He rode into town, reined in Eclipse in front of the sheriff's office.

"Did you find Willie?" he asked, surprising Murphy, who was seated behind his desk.

"Not yet. You find anything?"

"I lost the trail," Clint said, "but I had a run-in with some of the men on the Perryman ranch."

"They brace you?"

"They did," Clint said. "Tried to run me off."

Murphy sat back in his chair and asked, "And what happened?"

"I had to kill one of them."

"Who?"

"Fella named Kane."

"Kane?" Murphy said. "The foreman? I guess that doesn't surprise me. He's the type—or was."

"Pushy," Clint said. "I gave him every chance to back down, but he wouldn't."

"Well," Murphy said, "I guess I'll expect to hear from Mr. Perryman—probably through the mayor. They're friends."

"And I'll bet Perryman is one of his biggest supporters for reelection, right?"

"Not one of," the sheriff said. "The biggest."

"I told his men where he could find me," Clint said. "Will he come looking for me?"

"Yeah, he will," Murphy said, "and he won't waste any time either."

"Well," Clint said, "if he comes asking, you know where to find me."

"I do," Murphy said. "And don't worry. He'll be here."

Clint started for the door, then stopped.

"I've been meaning to ask you."

"Yeah?"

"Don't you have any deputies?"

"I used to," Murphy said, "but the mayor decided to cut the town budget to try and save the people some money. Guess where he started cuttin' first?"

"Right here," Clint said.

"You said it," Murphy said. "Both my deputies. Poof."

"I understand," Clint said. "What happened with that fellow you said was going to help you find Willie?"

"First I got to find him," Murphy said, "before I can find Willie."

Clint shook his head and left the office.

EIGHTEEN

From the sheriff's office Clint went to Maddy's whore-house to check on the boy. He was admitted by Cardwell, Lily's security man, and brought to her office.

"Well, there you are," she said. "I was beginning to think you had gone and left us with the boy."

"Not likely," Clint said. "I mean—I don't mean I wouldn't leave him with you, I mean I wouldn't leave—"

"I understand what you mean," she said, smiling. "No offense taken."

"How's he doing?"

"The girls are taking good care of him," she said. "Every-one's getting a turn."

"Where is he?"

"Upstairs," she said, rising out of her chair. "Let me show you."

She led the way from the office and up the steps to the second floor.

"Have you found out anything?" she asked as they walked along the hall.

"We know that his family was murdered," Clint said, "including his sister."

"Sister? How old?"

"Twelve maybe."

"Bastards," she said. "Who did it?"

"For now it looks like two men were hired," Clint said. "One of them is dead."

"How'd that happen?"

"I think his employer had him killed for leaving the boy alive."

"Why would somebody want to kill a small boy?" she asked.

"I don't know," he answered. "I'm still looking for someone to ask."

She opened a door and let him go in first. A skinny girl with long brown hair was seated on the floor with the boy, playing with him. When the boy saw Clint, he smiled, and ignored the girl. He reached his arms out toward Clint.

"He's missed you," the girl said.

"He doesn't even know me," Clint said.

"Look at him," Lily said. "He knows you. Go ahead and pick him up."

Clint walked to the boy, stooped, and picked him up. The boy's arms immediately went around his neck.

"Mama," the boy said.

"That's all he says," the brown-haired girl told him. "It's all he ever says."

"No," Clint said to the boy, "I'm not your mama." He bounced the boy a bit, until he laughed. "How you doing, huh? The girls treating you okay?"

"They're treating him like a little prince," Lily said, tickling the boy's chin. "Aren't they? My little prince?"

The boy giggled.

"Here you go," Clint said, putting the boy back down on the floor. "Play with your friend."

"Are you leaving already?" Lily asked.

"I just wanted to check on him," he said. "I've still got some searching to do."

"I'll take you back down, then."

Lily led him down to the front door and opened it for him.

"Do you know a man named Milton Perryman?" he asked.

"I know everybody in town," she said. "Yes, I know Perryman. Do you think he hired those men?"

"I have no idea," he said. "I just had a run-in with some of his men today. I had to kill one of them."

"Who?"

"Kane, the foreman."

"He probably pushed you into it."

"He did. You knew him, huh?"

"He was a customer," she said. "Most of the Perryman hands are."

"And Perryman?"

"He has a wife."

"I'll bet a lot of your customers have wives."

"Not like his," she said.

He started away and she grabbed his arm.

"If you're going up against Perryman—and you are, because you killed one of his men—you've got to be careful. Very careful. The man has no scruples."

"I will," he said. "Thanks for the warning."

He went out the door and she closed it behind him.

NINETEEN

Clint went to his hotel rather than stopping at the saloon. He was tired after being on horseback most of the day. Eclipse was being catered to at the livery stable, so why not him, as well? The hotel had a small dining room, which was empty, so he got good service. The steak was palatable, mostly because he was starving.

He was working on the steak and potatoes when he noticed Lily enter the dining room. This could not have been her choice for supper, so he determined she must be looking for him.

He waved at her. She spotted him and crossed the room, holding a shawl tightly around her. Other diners in the room watched her, but he noticed no one spoke to her. Men and women both turned their attention away.

"May I join you?" she asked.

"Of course," he said. He stood to hold her chair, and she thanked him. He noticed she also kept her eyes averted from the other diners.

"Why don't you look at them?" he asked, sitting across from her.

"Why frighten them?" she asked. "The men are all afraid

their wives will realize they know me. The women are afraid their men will greet me."

"You're a successful businesswoman in this town," he said.

"I'm a whore."

"You run a whorehouse," he said. "That doesn't make you a whore."

"An ex-whore, then," she said, "now a madam. Little difference to most of the women in Chester."

Clint waved a waiter over.

"Will you eat?" he asked.

She smiled.

"I was hoping to find you in your room," she admitted. "The clerk told me you were here. So yes, I'll eat with you."

The waiter came over and Lily ordered a chicken dinner. While he was there, the man poured her some coffee.

"Why were you looking for me?" Clint asked.

"The boy," she said. "What are your plans for him?"

"I'm not sure."

"You must have something in mind."

"The doctor," he replied, "says there are some families hereabouts who would take him, who want a child."

"And you wouldn't take him?" she asked.

"I told you," he said. "I'm no one's father."

"No desire to settle down?" she asked. "Have a family of your own?"

"No," he said. "Those days are long gone for me. I'll likely die in the saddle, at the wrong end of a bullet. I wouldn't want to leave a family behind to deal with that."

"What if you gave up your gun?"

He smiled.

"If I gave up my gun," he said, "I'd be dead the very next minute."

"Someone would kill you if you were unarmed?" she asked.

"They would stand in line for the privilege."

"It must be terrible to know that."

"Not if you accept it," he said.

"And you do?"

"I don't have much choice," Clint said. "It's been that way for a very long time."

"That's too bad."

"What about you?" he asked.

"What about me?"

"You accept the hand life has dealt to you, don't you?" he asked.

She stared at him for a few moments, then said, "I think I see what you mean."

The waiter came with her supper and they got down to the business of eating. Since Clint was already half done with his meal, he slowed down so that they'd finish and be ready for dessert around the same time.

After pie and coffee, Clint and Lily left the dining room and stepped into the hotel lobby.

"Going back to your house?" he asked.

"I don't think so."

"Do we have more to talk about?" he asked.

"When I said I was hoping to find you in your room," she told him, "I didn't mean to talk."

Clint looked around but nobody seemed to be paying much attention to them.

"Aren't you worried about your reputation?"

"It would probably damage my reputation if you sent me away," she said. "Unless you're not interested."

"Oh," he said, "I'm interested. Come on."

Walt Billings had a fine, unobscured view of Clint Adams and Lily from his position seated on a sofa in the lobby.

His boss had called him in just about an hour and a half ago, told him he wanted him to go to town and keep an eye on Clint Adams.

"Wait," he'd said, "the Gunsmith?"

"You got a problem with that?" Perryman had asked. "I don't pay you enough?"

"Well . . . well, yeah, you pay me good, but—"

"I'm not asking you to go up against the man," Perryman told him. "I just want to know where he is at all times, and who he talks to. Can you do that, Walt?"

"Sure, boss, sure," Billings had said. "I can do that."

And since Clint Adams had no idea who he was, he figured he could keep an eye on the man just fine from the lobby of his hotel.

So he watched as Adams and Lily walked to the stairs and went up to the second floor, where Billings assumed Clint Adams had his room.

And just to be sure, when the couple had disappeared, Billings got up and approached the front desk.

TWENTY

As they entered, she removed her shawl and said, "Well, you got the best room in the house."

"How do you know that?" he asked.

She gave him a sly smile and said, "I've been in this hotel before, Clint."

"Of course."

"But not for some time," she admitted. "I'm what's considered past my prime."

"Not from where I'm standing."

"You know that you're an unusual man, right?"

"Because of my gun?"

"No," she said, "because of who you are. Because of what you're doing for that baby."

"I'm doing what anybody would do."

"That's not true, at all," she said. She sat on the end of the bed and folded her hands in her lap. "I had to stop a lot of the girls from coming over here."

"A lot of them?"

"Well, one at a time. But they all feel you're a . . . singular kind of man. It makes you even more attractive."

"I'm flattered."

He walked to her and sat next to her.

She laughed.

"What is it?" he asked.

"I've done this a million times—well, not a million times—but a lot. Been with a man, I mean." She looked at him. "So why am I so nervous?"

"Maybe it's been a while."

"It has," she said. "I've been running Maddy's for eight years now."

"And in all that time . . . ?"

She shook her head.

"Not once."

"Why not?"

"After so many years . . . there has to be a connection, but there never has been . . . until now."

"Lily—"

She put her hand on his leg and said, "Don't get me wrong. I'm not expecting you to feel a connection. I'm only expecting you to feel one thing." She slid her hand up his thigh to his groin. "And I see I'm right." She squeezed.

He stood up and reached his hands out to her. She put hers in his and he pulled her to her feet and kissed her. He felt her trembling in his arms, her mouth eager beneath his.

She reached between them to unbuckle his gun belt. Before it could fall, he grabbed it, walked to the bedpost, and hung it there.

"Within easy reach?" she asked.

"Always."

She walked to him.

"You won't need that for me," she said, reaching for him.

Veronica Perryman entered the den, where her husband was sitting in a comfortable chair, holding a snifter of brandy.

"Are you coming to bed?" she asked.

"In a little while," he said. "Would you like some brandy?"

"No."

She was wearing a purple robe over her nightgown, belted tightly at the waist. He was still dressed.

"What are you thinking about?" she asked.

"The usual," he said. "Business."

"The boy?"

"Among other things."

"What are you going to do now that you know the Gunsmith is involved?"

"Tomorrow I'm going into town."

"To try to kill him?"

"To see him," he said. "Talk to him. See what he knows."

"What do you think he knows?"

"I have no idea," Perryman said. "That's why I want to talk to him."

"Who are you taking with you?"

"Kendall."

"That's all?"

"That's all I need to talk to him, Veronica," he answered.

"And then?" she asked, folding her arms. "After you find out what he knows?"

"Then I'll decide," Perryman said. "My whole career has been predicated on making informed decisions, my dear."

"Like the one you made about marrying me?"

He smiled and said, "Exactly."

"Milton," she said, dropping her arms to her sides, "you better be right."

"My dear," he said, "when will you learn that I'm always right?"

She just turned and left the room.

After his wife left, Perryman stood and poured himself some more brandy. He sat back down, swirled the amber liquid in the glass, and stared into it, as if it had properties that would help tell him the future.

It didn't.

It wasn't going to be quite that easy.

Upstairs in the room they shared, Veronica sat on the bed. She knew her husband thought he was always right, but she had her doubts. And she was not ready to give up everything they had just because he was stubborn.

That meant that she was going to have to take some steps of her own to make sure that didn't happen.

TWENTY-ONE

Lily was not only nervous, but shy about showing her body.

"Could we put the lights out first?" she said when Clint's hands began to work on her clothes.

"I want to see you," he said.

"That's just it," she said. "I don't want you to see me."

"You're a beautiful woman, Lily," he told her. "What have you got to be ashamed of?"

"I'm forty-five years old, Clint."

"You were confident enough to come here tonight," he said. "You knew you'd get into my room."

"Yes, but . . ."

"But what?"

"You're a man," she said. "Men will usually take whatever a woman is willing to give them—and more."

"Well," he said, lowering the top of her dress so that her breasts were bare, "I can assure you, you wouldn't be here unless I wanted you."

Her breasts were large, bottom heavy, with dark nipples that were already hard. He rubbed his palm over one nipple and she shivered, gooseflesh appearing all over.

"Still want the lights out?" he asked, cupping one breast in his hand.

"What lights?" she asked.

He smiled and kissed her, while his hands bared even more of her flesh . . .

Walt Billings started to get nervous about remaining in the hotel lobby. He determined that Clint Adams was, indeed, staying at that hotel. Adams had gone up to his room with Lily, the madam from Maddy's whorehouse, so what were the chances he'd be coming back down anytime soon? Probably slim, but Walt was still uncomfortable, especially when the place emptied out and it was just him and the desk clerk.

He decided to leave the hotel, but keep an eye on it from outside. His boss didn't give him a time limit for this job, and Billings certainly didn't have the wherewithal to make that kind of a decision for himself.

He figured to be at it all night.

Clint peeled Lily's clothes from her, and when she was completely naked, he laid her down on the bed.

Lily found his touch and his kisses incredibly tender, nothing she'd ever experienced before with a man. Most of the men she had ever been with had left behind bruises on her pale flesh. The only color change on her skin now was a red flush that covered her from head to toe. It had been such a long time since she'd felt anything akin to desire or passion for a man that it took her a little while to recognize them.

And when she did, she smiled.

Clint enjoyed Lily's body. She was a mature woman, and the extra flesh she wore did nothing to dampen his ardor. She was, in fact, exactly his type, and he was extremely pleased with how she felt and tasted.

Lily was submissive, didn't resist when he took over. He explored her body with his hands and mouth, from head to toe, before concentrating all his attention between her legs.

She moaned and gasped as he tongued her, enflamed her, until she was writhing beneath him uncontrollably. He mounted her then, even before the waves of pleasure began to wane, so that rather than fade, they simply transitioned into a whole new set . . .

"That was . . ." she said, trailing off.

"Nice," he said.

They were lying side by side on the bed, naked, he on his back and she balled up next to him, her arms encircling her knees.

"I was going to say it was like 'the first time,'" she went on. "I know that sounds idiotic for a woman of my age to say, but . . . see, my actual first time was . . . I was fourteen, and my father . . . sold me to this man to settle a debt. From that point on, I was just an . . . object. Later, he sold me to a whorehouse, and the rest is, well, history."

"So you've never enjoyed sex."

"No," she said, then reached out to touch him and added, "until now."

"I'm glad I could help."

"Oh, you did more than help," she said. She uncoiled now and stretched. "You've transformed me."

"Lily—"

"No, no," she said, "I don't just mean tonight. I mean the moment you walked into my place with that child and put him in my arms."

"Oh."

She rolled onto her stomach and looked at him, brushing the hair from her eyes.

"You two men," she said. "My life's never gonna be the same now."

"In what way?"

"Well, you'll leave, of course," she said, "and I'm thinking . . . I'm thinking of taking the boy myself."

"Ah," he said.

"Ah, indeed," she said. "A whore with a baby."

"I wasn't thinking that, at all."

"But everyone else will."

"What they think doesn't matter," Clint said.

"No," she said, "only what you think, because you're the one who can give him to me."

"Well, not legally."

"I'm not talking about legally," she said. "I mean, I know the West is much more civilized than it used to be, but who's going to care if you give me that baby?"

"Well, Doc Simon might have something to say about it."

"I don't think we'll have to worry about him," she said, stretching again. Before he could ask what she meant, she reached between his legs and said, "You're not tired, are you?"

As she stroked him to life, he said, "I think you know the answer to that."

TWENTY-TWO

While they didn't plan it, Lily ended up spending the night in Clint's room. They slept, woke, made love, slept, woke, made love . . . well, several times. By morning they were both pleasantly exhausted.

Clint watched while Lily got dressed.

"Sure you don't want to go downstairs for breakfast?" he asked her.

"I've got to get back," she said. "The girls will take time off if I'm not there. And I want to check on the baby."

"Are you really going to call him Happy?"

"Not after that clown remark you made," she said. "We're still trying to come up with a name."

"Well, pick carefully," Clint said. "The name might actually stick."

She walked to the bed and kissed him.

"Thank you, Clint."

"I think I should thank you."

"You know what I mean."

"Lily—"

"I'll see you again soon," she said, and left the room.

* * *

Kendall knocked on the door of the house that morning, was admitted by the housekeeper.

"Mr. Perryman is having breakfast," she said. "He wants you to wait here."

"All right," he said. "I'll just be in the living—"

"No," she said, "he was very specific that you wait right here, by the door."

Kendall studied her to see if she was telling the truth, then said, "Yeah, okay."

"I'll tell him you're here."

He nodded.

"What is it?" Perryman asked as the housekeeper entered the dining room.

"Mr. Kendall is here."

"Is he waiting?"

"Yes, sir. By the door, as you asked."

"Good. Thank you."

As she left, his wife leaned forward and asked, "Why don't you let him come in and have some breakfast?"

"I don't want to have breakfast with one of my ranch hands, dear," he said. "Besides, I'm sure he had breakfast in the bunkhouse."

"Well, how long will you make him wait?"

"Until I finish my breakfast."

She looked at his plate, which was almost empty.

"Can I persuade you to take more men?"

"Not this time," he said. "Don't worry, it will be fine."

"And the baby—"

"The boy will be dealt with."

"How?"

He put his napkin down and stood up.

"I don't think you want to know that."

"Milton—"

"You didn't want to know the details about the family,"

he reminded her. "So I'm sure you won't want to know this. I'll see you later."

He found Kendall waiting by the door.

"The horses outside?"

"Yes, sir."

"Let's go, then."

"Um . . ."

"What is it?"

"Do you think we need more men, sir?"

"We're only going to talk to the man, Kendall," Perryman said. "He's not going to shoot us."

"Are you sure?" Kendall asked. "I mean . . . that's what he does, ain't it?"

"Just do as I tell you and everything will be fine," Perryman said. "All right?"

"Yes, sir," Kendall said. "All right."

Clint got dressed and went down for breakfast. It was just easier to have it right there in the hotel. Once again his meal was interrupted as Sheriff Murphy walked in and approached his table.

"Coffee?" Clint asked.

"Definitely."

Murphy sat down.

"How about breakfast?"

"I had something . . . oh, all right." He looked at the waiter. "Bacon and eggs."

"Sure, Sheriff."

Clint poured Murphy a cup of coffee and went back to his meal.

"Find Willie?" Clint asked.

"Not yet."

"Could he have left town?"

"Where would he go?"

"Into hiding?"

"Willie doesn't know anyplace else," Murphy said. "If he's hidin', he doin' it in town."

"Maybe I should help you look," Clint said, "go door-to-door."

Murphy shrugged and said, "Why not, but if I was you, I'd expect a visit from Milton Perryman today."

"If that does happen," Clint assured him, "I'll be ready for him."

TWENTY-THREE

Milton Perryman and his man, Kendall, rode into town an hour later. Clint and the sheriff were just coming out of the hotel. They had taken their time over breakfast.

"There he is," Sheriff Murphy said.

"Perryman?"

"Yeah."

Clint watched the two men ride by.

"That man with him," he said, "he was one of the men who braced me. He was there when I had to kill the foreman."

"Looks like they're headin' for my office."

"I tell you what," Clint said, grabbing a chair, "you go and talk to them and I'll wait right here. You bring them over to me."

"Is there gonna be any trouble?" Murphy asked.

"Not on my part," Clint assured him. "I'm not looking for any trouble."

"Yeah, okay," Murphy said. "I'll bring 'em over."

Clint sat down in the chair and watched as Murphy crossed the street and walked to his office. From his vantage point he could see that the two men had reined in their horses in front of the sheriff's office.

He settled into his chair to wait.

*   *   *

As Murphy entered his office, Perryman and his man, Kendall, turned to face him.

"There you are, Sheriff," Perryman said.

"Mr. Perryman."

"I don't know if you're aware of it, but one of my men was killed yesterday. My foreman, Kane."

"I heard," Murphy said, moving around behind his desk.

"We know who did it. Kendall here was a witness."

"So do I."

"So what are you going to do about it?"

"Nothin'."

"Why not?" Perryman asked. "Are you afraid of the Gunsmith?"

"Not at all," the lawman said. "In fact, I just had breakfast with him. He's a very pleasant fellow."

"If you know the Gunsmith killed Kane, why aren't you arresting him?"

"Because Kane pressed him," Murphy said, "forced his hand. He had no choice."

"Why do you believe that?"

"Because I knew Kane," Murphy said. "You did, too, Mr. Perryman. You know it's true. Kendall here must've told you."

Kendall kept conspicuously quiet, glanced over at his boss.

"You're probably right," Perryman said finally. "I guess I'd better talk to the man myself. Do you have a problem with that?"

"Not at all."

"Can you tell me where he is?"

"You passed him on the way into town," Murphy said. "He's sitting in front of the hotel up the street."

"The hotel."

"That's right."

"Well," Perryman said, "I'm going to walk over there and have a talk with him."

"That's fine."

"I suppose he knows I'm coming?"

"He does."

"You told him?"

"Yeah."

Perryman turned, walked to the door, then turned back.

"I guess I'm going to have to talk to the mayor about your job, Sheriff."

"You do that, Mr. Perryman," Murphy said. "If you find somebody else who wants this job, you let me know."

Perryman went out the door.

Kendall turned and looked at the lawman.

"Aw, Murphy," he said.

"Don't do anything stupid, Kendall," Murphy said.

"I'll try not to."

He followed his boss out the door, and up the street.

Clint saw the two men walking toward him. They had left their horses behind, in front of the sheriff's office. He sat back in the chair and watched them, his hand down by his gun.

The older man he assumed was Perryman mounted the boardwalk and approached. The other man—the one he recognized—stood behind and to the right. He looked nervous.

"Mr. Adams?"

"That's right."

"I'm Milton Perryman."

"Mr. Perryman."

"You killed one of my men yesterday."

"He didn't give me much of a choice."

"That may be so," Perryman said, "but you understand I can't let something like that go without reprisal."

"Reprisal?"

"Unless you leave town," Perryman went on, "today."

"I can't do that."

"Why not?"

"I have unfinished business," Clint said. "You see, someone killed a family a few days ago, and I found the last surviving member. A little boy. And now he's my responsibility. Do you understand that?" Clint suddenly knew that this man had something to do with the massacre of the boy's family. "My responsibility. That means I won't let anything happen to him. Do you understand?"

"And why would I have to understand that, Mr. Adams?" Perryman asked. "I know nothing of such things. The only murder I know of is you killing my foreman. Take my advice. Leave town."

"Take my advice," Clint said. "Confess what you did, turn yourself in. It's the only way you'll be safe from me."

"Is that a threat?"

"No threat," Clint said. "Just fact."

TWENTY-FOUR

Clint entered the sheriff's office.

"What?" Murphy said. "I didn't hear any shots."

"He did it," Clint said.

"Did what?"

"He had that family killed," Clint said.

"Are you sure?"

"I feel it."

"So you're not sure."

"No, I'm sure," Clint said, "I just can't prove it. For that we need Willie."

"What did you say to him?"

"That if he tries to harm that child, he'll have to go through me."

"And what did he say?"

"He advised me to leave town."

Murphy rubbed his face with his hands.

"This ain't gonna end well," he said.

"For who?"

"Any of us," Murphy said. "Perryman's gonna talk to the mayor about my job."

"You're not going to lose your job."

"Oh no? Why not?"

"Because I'm going to talk to the mayor."

"What are you gonna say to him?"

"I have no idea," Clint said. "Give me a break. I just came up with the idea."

Mayor Jimmy Lennon had a mouthful of lemon pie when he saw Milton Perryman walking toward him.

"Excellent," he said to the woman in front of him. "That is excellent pie. Thank you so much."

"You're welcome, Mayor," the woman said. "You have my vote."

"And you have mine," Lennon said. "I'll be sending people over here to your little café."

"Thank you."

"Jimmy—" Perryman stared, but Lennon cut him off.

"Not here! Outside!"

The mayor pushed Perryman out to the boardwalk and glared up at the older man.

"I'm working here, Milton," he said. "What do you want?"

"I want you to get rid of that useless sheriff," Perryman said, "and I want Clint Adams run out of town."

"Those are not the kinds of things I want to be concerned with during an election, Milton."

"Well, you better consider it, if you want to keep my support," Perryman said. "Adams killed my foreman, and your sheriff is doing nothing about it. And now the man has threatened me."

"Threatened how?"

"He threatened to kill me!"

"All right, okay," Lennon said, "relax, take it easy. I'll have a talk with Murphy about it."

"You better do more than talk, Jimmy," Perryman said. "If you don't get Adams out of town, I'm not going to be a target for him. I'll have him taken care of myself."

"Milton," Lennon said, "just leave it with me, all right?

Get out of town today, go back home, and wait for hear from me."

"I'll go home," Perryman said, "but I'm not going to just wait. I'm going to get ready."

He turned and stormed away, with Kendall trotting along after him.

Lennon turned, briefly considered going back into the café, but he was afraid they'd make him have another bite of that horrible lemon pie, so he walked away and headed for his next appointment.

"Let me tell you about Mayor Jimmy Lennon," Murphy said to Clint. "He's young, in his thirties, and he's ambitious."

"That's the only kind of politician I've ever met," Clint told him.

"Yeah, well," Murphy said, "he's got his own ways of gettin' things done."

"How's that?"

"He's got his own private security," Murphy said. "He don't take them around with him when he's campaigning, but they're usually within earshot. You better watch out for them."

"Is it an official security force?" Clint asked. "Do they have legal powers?"

"No," Murphy said, "he pays them out of his own pocket—supposedly."

"Meaning he steals money from the town to pay them."

"It'd be hard to try and prove that, but yeah, that's what I mean."

"Okay then," Clint said, "I'll keep that in mind when I talk to him. What about him and Perryman?"

"Perryman is the mayor's biggest supporter," Murphy said, "and I'm talkin' about money."

"I understand."

"I hope you do."

Clint headed for the door, then stopped.

"How far can I depend on you, Sheriff?"

"I'll uphold the law," Murphy said. "I'll do the job I'm paid to do."

"That's all I ask," Clint said. "Where do you think I can find the mayor now?"

"He's probably out campaigning," Murphy said, "kissing babies and shaking hands."

"Well," Clint said, "wherever he is, I'll find him."

Instead of going home, as he had told the mayor he would, Milton Perryman headed for the Crystal Chandelier. It was the biggest, most expensive saloon in town, where the rich ranchers and wealthy businessmen in town drank.

He went through the batwing doors, then turned abruptly and put his hand against Kendall's chest.

"Not you," he said.

Kendall was disappointed. He'd never been in the Crystal Chandelier before.

"B-But—"

"You ride back to the ranch and get some men."

"Who?"

"Whoever can handle a gun," Perryman said, "and won't mind making some bonus money."

"How many?"

"Half a dozen."

"O-Okay."

"And find me Jess Bowen," Perryman called after his man, "and have him meet me here."

Sure, Kendall thought, Bowen gets to see the inside of the Crystal.

"Yes, sir," he said.

Perryman turned, headed for his usual table, and waved to one of the saloon girls.

TWENTY-FIVE

Clint walked around town, still noticing the VOTE FOR LENNON signs, and listening to some of the incumbent's supporters preaching his virtues. He wondered if these men—all armed with what appeared to be well-maintained pistols—were part of the mayor's private security force.

He saw a crowd gathered in front of a building, crossed the street to see if it was a campaign stop for the mayor. It was a dress shop, and he saw a man in a dark suit standing in the midst of a group of women of all ages, smiling and doffing his hat.

"Yes, ladies," he said, "if elected, I promise to continue to make the streets of Chester safe for all of you to walk safely and unmolested, no matter what time of day it is."

The women all liked that and applauded the man. He looked over their heads and saw Clint watching him. Clint thought he was the youngest and fittest town mayor he'd ever seen. That obviously didn't hurt when it came to getting the female vote.

"All right, ladies," the mayor said, "I must move on now. Have a good day."

He waded through the crowd of women until he was standing in front of Clint.

"Are you Clint Adams?"

"I am," Clint said. "You were expecting me?"

"I heard talk you were in town," he said. "Can I buy you a drink, sir?"

"Why not? But you know I can't vote."

"I just think we should have a talk."

"Suits me."

"That saloon across the street okay?"

"It's your town."

"It's never very full and I won't have to do much glad-handing. Come on."

The two men walked across the street and entered the small saloon. The mayor was right—there were only a few men in the place, and none of them seemed to want to shake his hand. They got a beer each and sat at a table.

"I guess these aren't your supporters," Clint said.

"I think I'll manage to get along without their votes," Mayor Lennon said.

Clint sipped his beer and waited. This conversation was the mayor's idea. Clint figured to let him take the lead.

"I understand you've killed a man since your arrival."

"You talked with Milton Perryman."

"He came to me, yes," Lennon said. "He said you killed his foreman, and threatened him."

"I killed his foreman, yes," Clint said. "He didn't give me any choice, and there were witnesses to that."

"Perryman's men."

"Yes."

"Not very reliable witnesses in your eyes."

"Probably not."

"What about the threat?"

"I didn't threaten the man," Clint said. "I stated a fact."

"That you're going to kill him?"

"Do you know the reason I'm in town in the first place?" Clint asked.

"I do not."

"Then let me fill you in . . ."

The mayor listened to Clint's story without comment, didn't speak until he had finished.

"So you think Perryman had something to do with those people's deaths? And that he's a danger to the surviving child?"

"That's what I think."

"Can you prove it?"

"No," Clint said, "but the promise I made was that I'd kill him if he tried to harm that child."

"And where is the child now?"

Clint hesitated.

"Do you believe I am a threat to the child?" Lennon asked.

Clint hesitated again, then said, "No, but I don't think there's any reason for you to know where he is at the moment."

Lennon raised one hand and said, "Granted. But I hope you're not thinking of taking your suspicions to the street to prove them."

"If my suspicions turn out to be true, I'll take them to the law," Clint said. "The only way they'll end up on the street is if Perryman drags them there."

"Well," Lennon said, "I have an election to be concerned with, and one of my campaign promises is to keep the streets safe."

"You better have a heart-to-heart with your friend Perryman, then."

"He's not my friend," Lennon said, "but he is an important man in this town, and I will be talking with him. I'll assure him that you have no plans to kill him in the near future."

"Unless he pushes me into it."

"I understand." Lennon finished his beer. "I'm afraid I have to get back to the streets right now."

"Why campaign so hard when you don't have an opponent?" Clint asked.

Lennon stood up.

"I don't like to take anything for granted, Mr. Adams."

Clint leaned back in his chair and watched the mayor leave the saloon. He had a mouthful of beer left in his mug. So he tossed that back and briefly considered having another. He thought a moment about the conversation with the mayor, and didn't see that it had accomplished anything for either of them. But if Perryman was as big a supporter as he'd been told, it made sense to assume that the mayor would do whatever was best for Milton Perryman—and for himself.

That meant that Clint Adams had to do what was best for him, and for the boy.

Milton Perryman looked up as the big man came through the batwing doors. Others looked at him as well, for Jess Bowen was not a regular customer there. In fact, Bowen had never been inside the place before. He looked around, saw Perryman, and walked to his table.

"You lookin' for me?" Bowen asked.

"Do you want to make some money?"

"I always wanna make some money."

"Then sit down," Perryman said. "Beer?"

"Yeah."

Perryman waved and a saloon girl came rushing over.

"Bring my friend a beer."

"Yes, sir."

Bowen sat back and looked the place over. His eyes lingered on the collection of crystal chandeliers that dotted the ceiling.

"Nice place," he said.

"Yes, it is."

The girl appeared with the beer, and Bowen promptly drank half of it down.

"Okay," he said, "let's get down to business."

"You know Willie Delvin?"

"I do."

"Do you have any problem with killing him?"

"Killin' Willie?" Bowen asked. "I think I'd kinda like that."

"Well," Perryman said, "here's what I want . . ."

TWENTY-SIX

By the time Clint got out to the street, the mayor was out sight. Clint wasn't sure about his next move, and was about to head for his hotel when he saw Sheriff Murphy coming his way.

"Did you have your meetin' with the mayor?" the lawman asked.

"I did," Clint said, "although it wasn't very fruitful, I'm afraid."

"Well," Murphy said, "between you and Perryman, I think I know which way the mayor would lean."

"So he's Perryman's man?" Clint said.

"It's probably the other way around," Murphy said, "but listen, I was looking for you because I may have an idea where Willie is."

"An idea?"

"Well, more than an idea," Murphy said. "Somebody told me he's holed up in a house outside of town."

"You want to go and see if it's a fact?"

"That's why I'm here."

"Lead the way, then."

* * *

Murphy told Clint that while the house was outside of town, it was within walking distance. When they reached it, they stopped a few yards away to take a look.

There was a corral next to a falling-down one-room house, with one horse in it.

"Let's check the horse," Clint said.

"Right."

They moved quickly to the corral, where Clint went inside and checked the horse's hoof.

"This is the horse," Clint said. "If it's not Willie inside, it's somebody I'm interested in."

"I guess we should just go and find out."

The house was too small to have a back door, so they both approached the front, and then Clint kicked it in. They went in quickly, the sheriff holding his gun in his hand.

Willie was there.

Murphy walked to the body, knelt down, and checked it.

"He's dead," he said.

"Is it Willie?"

"Yup."

"How?"

"Shot."

"Damn," Clint said. "He was my last good chance to find out who hired him and his partner to kill that family."

Murphy stood up and holstered his gun.

"So what are you going to do now?"

"Well," Clint said, "with my best chances gone, I'll have to make the best of my worst ones."

They went back to town and split up. Murphy went to get himself some men and a buckboard to retrieve Willie's body.

They had searched the body and the house, but found nothing that would help determine who hired Willie, or who killed him.

Clint went to No. 8 and had a beer. At the bar he wondered if Willie had been killed by the people who hired him—which, to his mind, meant Perryman's men—or maybe the mayor's security force—but again, at the behest of Milton Perryman.

He finished his beer and walked over to City Hall. He didn't go inside, but took up position across the street. He wanted to see if he could spot any of the mayor's security men. He hadn't seen any with the mayor when he was campaigning with the group of women, but they may just have been keeping back out of sight.

As he watched, the mayor returned, and this time he had two men with him. They were wearing trail clothes rather than any sort of security uniform, but they were his men. They let the mayor go in ahead of them, looked around quickly, then followed. They were so focused on the mayor that they missed seeing Clint, watching from across the street.

He heard a buckboard coming down the street, looked over, and saw two men on it, with Sheriff Murphy riding alongside. He stepped out into the street.

"You mind if I come along?" he asked. "I want to take another look at the ground around the house and the corral."

"Be my guest," Murphy said. "Hop aboard."

Clint hopped into the bed of the buckboard and they started off again.

When they reached the house, Murphy told the men to stop the buckboard a few yards away.

"Go ahead and take your look around," Murphy said. "We'll go in and get the body ready to move."

Clint walked around the corral first. It hadn't been used in a long time, so the horse that was inside had left the only recent tracks. He walked around the outside of the corral, still found no other tracks.

He moved to the house.

Sheriff Murphy stepped out, said, "They're wrapping the body in a blanket. Anything?"

"Not at the corral," Clint said, "but I've got tracks here made by two horses."

"Anything unusual about them?"

"Not that I can see." Clint went down to one knee for a better look. "I think one of these horses was carrying a heavy man. A big man." He pointed. "In fact, it's a pony, a small horse with a big man on it." He looked at Murphy. "That ring a bell?"

"Oh yeah," Sheriff Murphy said, nodding his head, "that rings a bell."

TWENTY-SEVEN

They went back to town, dropped the body off at the undertaker's, and then went to the sheriff's office. There was a pot of coffee waiting, and they each had a cup.

"Tell me about the big man," Clint said.

"It's a joke in town," Murphy said. "His name's Jess Bowen, and he rides a mustang. His feet almost touch the ground on either side when he rides."

"That means he's . . ."

"That's right," the sheriff said. "He's nearly seven feet tall."

"There were some big footprints in front of the house, too."

"Then it had to be him."

"Is he part of the mayor's security?"

"No," Murphy said.

"Then he works for Perryman?"

"No."

"Then . . . who does he work for?"

"Anybody who'll pay him, like Willie."

"So then somebody hired him to kill Willie."

"Probably."

"But who?"

"We're in the same situation as we were with Willie," Murphy said. "We'll need to find Jess to ask him."

"Do you know where he lives?"

"No," Murphy said. "Nobody does. I think he just lies down wherever he is when he gets tired."

"What about eating?"

"He manages."

"So when you see him around town, what's he doing?"

"Usually," Murphy said, "he's ridin' in or ridin' out. For a big man, he moves real quietly."

"So I just have to go out and see if I spot him."

"I guess."

"Does he have a friend?"

Murphy thought a moment, then brightened and said, "Maybe just one."

"Who?"

"His name's Caleb Stone."

"And what's Caleb do?"

"Well," Murphy said, "I guess you'd call him the town drunk."

When trying to find the town drunk, you at least had some idea of where to look.

"Where's he drink?" Clint asked.

"Everywhere," Murphy said. "Every saloon."

"The Crystal Chandelier?"

"No, not there," Murphy said. "They don't let him in. But everywhere else. So I guess if anyone knows where Jess lives, it'll be Caleb."

"Then we've got to find Caleb."

"Let's just hope we find him alive."

"Who would want to kill him?"

Murphy shrugged. "Nobody," he said. "Unless somebody else figures out he's our only way to find Jess Bowen."

"Then we'd better find him before that happens."

* * *

They left the office and split up to check the saloons, or anyplace else Caleb could get a drink. That made Clint think of Maddy's. He decided to check there first, and look in on the boy at the same time. And Lily.

"Oh, it's you," Cardwell said when he opened the door. "I suppose you want to see Lily?"

"I want to see the boy," Clint said, "and talk to Lily, yes."

"Yeah, well, you better come in."

Clint wondered what was between Lily and Cardwell, and if the man knew about what was now between Lily and Clint.

"Cardwell," Clint said inside, "do know Caleb Stone?"

"The drunk? Sure. Why?"

"Does he ever come here?"

"No," Cardwell said. "Lily doesn't allow him in here. He's always drunk, and he smells. None of the girls wanna touch him."

"I can't blame them, if that's the case," Clint said.

"You wanna see Lily? Or the boy?"

"The boy."

"Come on."

Clint followed Cardwell up the stairs to a different room than last time. The boy was on the bed, playing with two of the girls.

"I'll get Lily," Cardwell said.

Clint nodded and the man left the room.

"How's he doing, girls?" he asked.

"He's great," one girl, a small brunette, said. "He's such a happy boy."

"What about you, handsome?" the other girl, a redhead, asked. "Are you a happy boy?" She got up, approached him, and put her hands on his arm. "Or do you wanna be?"

"I'll have to pass, I'm afraid," Clint said. "I'm just here to check on him."

"He's good," she said, "but I should go and get him something to drink."

She left, leaving Clint alone with the brunette and the boy. Clint moved to the bed and got down on one knee.

"How you doing, buddy?" he asked, reaching his hand out. The boy grabbed his thumb and held on tight. "Yeah, you're doing good. Whatever they're feeding you is doing you good."

"He's doing great," Lily said as she entered the room. "But he's really happy to see you."

She knelt down next to him, pressed her hip to his.

"What brings you here?" she asked. "Just checking on your boy?"

"I had some questions about Caleb Stone."

"Stone. He's not allowed in here."

"That's what Cardwell told me."

"Yeah, well, he smells. Why are you looking for him?"

"There are just some questions I have for him," Clint said. He eased his thumb out of the boy's grip and stood up. "I've got to go."

"You want Caleb Stone, you better check the saloons."

"I intend to," he said. "I just thought I'd start here and check on the boy."

They went out into the hall.

"Just on the boy?" she asked him.

Clint looked up and down the empty hallway, then kissed Lily quickly.

"I'll see you later?" she asked.

As they went down the stairs, he asked, "What's going on with you and your man, Cardwell?"

"Nothing," she said. "He works for me, that's all."

"Does he know that's all?"

She smiled and said, "He knows."

"Okay then," he said at the door. "I'll see you later on tonight."

As he went out the door, she called out, "Don't get yourself killed before then."

"I'll do my best."

Cardwell watched from a window as Clint left the house, then turned and said to one of the girls, "If Lily's lookin' for me, tell her I had somethin' personal to take care of."

"Well, okay," the girl said as he headed for the back door, "but you're gonna get yourself fired!"

TWENTY-EIGHT

Clint checked a few of the saloons, and the hotels that had saloons. Of course they knew Caleb Stone, but none of them had seen him recently.

Before he returned to the sheriff's office, he got an idea, changed direction, and stopped in at the mercantile store, which he figured sold whiskey by the bottle.

As he entered, two women were off to one side, looking at a bolt of cloth, and there was a man picking out a cigar.

"Be right with you, sir," the middle-aged man behind the counter said.

"That's okay," Clint said. "These ladies are before me."

The two women—one young, one middle-aged—looked over at him and smiled. He touched the brim of his hat.

"Come on, Randy," the clerk said, "pick out a cigar already. I got other customers."

"I can't rush my decision, George," the customer said. "A man's cigar is a serious thing."

"Well, these ladies are waiting to buy some cloth," the clerk said. "That's as serious to them as your cigar is to you."

The customer, Randy, turned to the women and said, "I'm sorry, ladies. I just ain't ready to make a decision."

"That's all right, sir," the older women said. "We're not

quite ready either." She looked at the clerk. "George, perhaps you can take care of this young man until we're ready."

The clerk looked at Clint.

"Are you better at makin' decisions than these people are, mister?"

"I don't have a decision to make," Clint said. "Just some questions to ask."

"Well, that oughtta be easy, then," George said. "What's your questions?"

"Do you know Caleb Stone?"

"I see him around," George said.

"Has he been in here recently? Maybe to buy a bottle of whiskey?" Clint asked.

"Mister," the other man, Randy, said, "if you knew Caleb, you'd know he ain't never bought a bottle of whiskey in his life."

"Randy's right," George said. "Caleb don't buy his whiskey. At least, not here."

"Then you haven't seen him lately?"

"Nope."

"You?" Clint asked Randy.

"Can't say I have."

"Then I guess I wasted your time, and mine," Clint said. "Sorry."

As he was leaving, Clint heard George saying, "Now, Randy, goddamnit, pick out a cigar."

He had walked only about half a block when he heard someone behind him.

"Mister?"

He turned, saw the young girl trotting toward him.

"Can I help you?"

"No," she said, "but maybe I can help you. My mama told me not to say nothin', but . . ."

"Say nothing about what?"

"Well, Caleb Stone."

"What about him?" he asked.

"Why do you want him?"

"I just have to ask him a few questions."

"About what?"

"Why does that concern you?" he asked.

"Because if I'm gonna help you, I have to know why."

"A man was killed," Clint said. "I'm trying to help the sheriff find out who did it."

"He's just a harmless drunk," she said. "He wouldn't kill anybody."

"We think Caleb might know something about it, that's all," Clint said.

"Well, I've seen him recently."

"Where?"

"Around my house," she said. "I mean, me and Ma's house."

"Now, why would he be around your house?"

"That's easy," she said. "He's my pa."

TWENTY-NINE

"Ma kicked him out when his drinkin' got too bad," the girl said as she led Clint to her house. She said her name was Tina Stone, and she was seventeen years old. "He's an embarrassment to her, but he sneaks back sometimes to see me."

"He's not an embarrassment to you?"

"He's my pa," she said. "I love him."

"Then why are you showing me where he is?"

"I'm thinking maybe if he helps you find a killer, he might feel worth something and stop drinking." She touched his arm. "Do you think I'm bein' silly?"

He did, but he said, "No, you're not being silly. You just love your pa and want him to get better."

"Yeah, that's what I think," she said. "That he's sick, and he needs to get better."

Clint knew that wasn't the case with drunks. It wasn't a sickness; it was a weakness. But in that case, maybe her plan would work after all.

Their house was one of a cluster of similar two-story homes that were fairly well kept.

"We have a small barn—actually, more of a lean-to—

behind our house," she said. "Sometimes he sleeps there—
or sleeps it off."

When they reached the house, Clint said, "Maybe you
should stay here—"

"I think it would be better if I went with you," she said.
"He might run from you."

His first instinct was to argue, but then he had second
thoughts.

"All right," he said. "Lead the way."

They went around the house to the back, where Clint
saw what she meant. It could hardly be called a barn.
While it was well cared for, it was still small, more—as
she said—a lean-to than anything else. From what he
could tell, there were no animals in it at the moment.

"Do you have a horse?" he asked.

"No," she said. "We did, but Pa sold it for . . ."

"Whiskey money?"

She lowered her head and said, "Yes."

"Okay," he said, "why don't you approach first and see
if he's in there?"

"A-All right."

He hung back while she approached the structure.

"Pa? You in there, Pa?" she called.

There was no answer, but she kept calling out as she got
closer. Clint suddenly realized that he might have sent her
in there to find her father dead.

He started forward.

"Pa?" she called, and stuck her head inside.

Clint was almost there when she came back out and
looked at him. He couldn't read the look on her face.

"Tina—"

"He's there," she said.

"Is he—"

"He's dead drunk," she said.

He hoped that she was right, and that her father was
only dead drunk, and not dead.

* * *

When Bowen entered the Crystal again, he attracted more attention only because there were more people there as it got later in the day.

"It's done," Bowen said, taking the seat across from Perryman.

"I heard," Perryman said. "The word had already gotten around that he was found. His body's at the undertaker's. Where have you been? Why did I have to hear it as gossip?"

"I had somethin' else to do."

"What?"

"There was just somebody else I had to see."

"I'm paying you," Perryman reminded him.

"I know that," Bowen said. "The job is done. What do you want now?"

"I want you to stay in town," Perryman said. "I have some other men, and I may need you to take the lead with them."

"Take the lead on what?"

"You know a man named Clint Adams?"

"The Gunsmith?"

"That's right."

Bowen smiled.

"I think I need another beer."

Clint leaned over the prone man and touched his shoulder.

"Caleb."

Nothing.

He shook him. If he didn't move, then he'd have to feel for a pulse.

"Caleb!"

"Pa?" Tina said.

After a moment the man groaned, and rolled over.

"Papa!" Tina said again, this time with relief.

"Tina?" he said, squinting. "Wha—what happened?"

"You were sleeping one off," Clint said.

Caleb looked at Clint.

"Who are you?"

"Clint Adams."

"What are you—what do you want?"

"Just to talk to you," Clint said. He looked at Tina. "Can we go inside?"

Before she could answer, Caleb sat up and said, "Better not. Her mother would skin me alive."

"Any water around?" Clint asked.

"Inside," Tina said, "and there's a well in the back."

"I'll get a bucket of water," Clint said. He looked at Caleb. "Don't run."

"Why would I run?" Caleb asked.

"I'll make sure he stays," Tina said.

Clint nodded, then left the lean-to to find the well. As he left, he heard Caleb ask again, "Why would I run?"

THIRTY

Clint brought back a bucket of water and promptly dunked Caleb's head into it.

"Ooh-wee," Caleb said, shaking water off his head. He rubbed his hands over his face.

"Can you concentrate?" Clint asked.

"On what?"

"I need your help."

"Okay, with what?"

"Jess Bowen."

Caleb suddenly looked scared. Maybe he and Bowen weren't exactly friends.

"Whataya want with Jess?"

"I need to talk to him."

"You ain't told me who you are."

"My name's Clint Adams."

Caleb was still sitting on the floor. At the sound of the name he skittered back until he was against one wall.

"Pa, what is it?" Tina asked.

"He's the Gunsmith."

Tina looked at Clint.

"Are you?"

"Yes."

"Don't kill me," Caleb said.

"Why would I do that?"

"Ain't that what you do?"

"No."

"He ain't no killer, Pa," Tina said. "I can tell. He's tryin' to find a killer."

"Who got killed?" Caleb asked.

"Willie Delvin."

"Willie's dead? When?"

"Earlier today."

Clint looked outside the lean-to. It was starting to get dark.

"Why are you looking for Jess?"

"We think he might know something about it."

"Or maybe he did it?"

"Maybe."

"Why you askin' me about him?"

"We heard you were friends."

Caleb snorted. "We ain't friends."

"But you know him. People have seen you together."

"He makes me run errands for him."

"Do you know where to find him?"

"Sometimes."

"Can you take me to someplace he might be?"

Suddenly, instead of looking frightened, Caleb had a cunning look in his eyes.

"What's in it for me?"

"We're gonna what?" Murphy asked.

"Pay him."

"Why?"

"Because it's easier than taking him into your cell block and beating it out of him."

Caleb was sitting in a chair in front of the sheriff's desk. Clint and Murphy were in the cell block, keeping their voices down.

"He claims he and Bowen aren't friends."

"Then why doesn't he just help us find him?"

"Because he wants to get something back for his trouble."

"So buy him a drink," Murphy said. "He'll usually do anythin' for a drink."

"He wants a little more than that."

"I ain't got much money," Murphy said. "Thirty a month and found don't do much for me."

"I'll pay him," Clint said.

"Well, if that's the case, what are we arguin' about?" Murphy said. "Let's just do it."

"Okay."

They went back into the office.

"Okay, Caleb, you got a deal," Clint said.

"Thanks," Caleb said, standing. He wiped his hands on his thighs. "Pay up."

"After I find Jess Bowen," Clint said.

"You plan on takin' him alive?"

"Yes," Clint said. "We need to talk to him."

"About what?"

"About who hired him to kill Willie."

"What do you care about Willie?" Caleb asked.

"It's too complicated to explain, Caleb," Clint said. "Just tell us where to find him."

"Well, I can't tell ya," Caleb said. "I'll have to show ya."

"So show us."

He licked his lips nervously.

"H-He can't know I talked to ya," Caleb said, "that I helped ya. Or he'll kill me."

"Once we find him," Murphy said, "he ain't gonna kill nobody ever again."

"Are ya sure?"

"Do you know who this man is?" Murphy asked, pointing at Clint.

"Well, yeah . . ."

"You think your friend Bowen can take him with a gun?"

"He ain't my friend," Caleb said, "but no, I don't. But with his hands—"

"He ain't gonna get close enough to do anythin' with his hands," Murphy assured him.

"Okay, Caleb," Clint said, "that's it. Let's go."

"I need—I need a drink before we get started."

"No."

"Just a small one," Caleb said. "I gotta have a small one. Just ta hold me."

Clint looked at Murphy.

"You got any whiskey?"

Murphy nodded, opened a drawer, and took out a half-full bottle. Clint went to the stove and got a coffee mug. He took the bottle and poured about one finger of whiskey into it.

"This is all you get," he told Caleb, holding the mug.

"Yeah, yeah, okay," Caleb said, holding his hands out.

Clint handed him the mug. He took it in both hands and greedily drank down the whiskey. Then he wiped out the bottom of the cup with his finger and licked it. It was a pathetic sight.

Clint took the mug back and handed the bottle to Murphy, who put it away. Caleb's eyes followed it all the way back into the drawer.

"Okay," Clint said, "where's Bowen?"

"I got—I got a coupla ideas."

"Fine," Clint said. "Lead the way."

"You both comin'?"

"We're both comin'," Murphy said.

"You plannin' on arrestin' Jess?"

"If I have to."

"He won't be easy to take."

"You let us worry about that, Caleb," Clint said. "You just concentrate on finding him."

Jess Bowen listened to what Milton Perryman wanted, drinking his beer and waiting for the man to finish.

"You got any problems with that?" the rancher asked.

"No problem at all."

"How long do you think it will take you to get set up?" Perryman asked.

"Not long," Bowen said. "In fact, I already got an idea."

"That's good," Perryman said.

"I'll need to bring in some other men."

"I don't have a problem with that," Perryman said. "We'll work out a price, and you pay them out of your take. Agreed?"

"Agreed," Bowen said. "Where will you be?"

"I'm heading back to my ranch tonight," Perryman said. "When the job is done, you'll find me there."

"How much can I get up front?" Bowen asked. "I might have to pay some people first."

Perryman took out a fat wallet.

"I can give you an advance now." He started taking money from his wallet and laying it on the table, bill by bill. Bowen then scooped it up and put it in his pocket, without fear that anyone in the place would try to rob him. Nobody would dare try.

"Okay," he said, standing up. "You'll be hearin' from me soon."

Perryman picked up the last of his beer, raised the mug, and said, "I look forward to it."

THIRTY-ONE

"If Jess is in any of the places I think he might be," Caleb said, "you won't be able to miss him."

They were walking down the main street, which was empty at night—at least, when compared to what it looked like during the day. There were some people strolling, a few others walking with purpose, either returning home or heading for a saloon. And from most of the saloons came light, and music, and voices.

"You gonna look in some of these saloons?" Murphy asked.

"Naw," Caleb said, "Jess Bowen wouldn't be in any of them. You know Warden's Saloon?"

"Jay Warden's place? Is that still open?"

"It's open," Caleb said, "to a few people."

"Like Bowen?"

"Exactly like Bowen."

"Where is this place?" Clint asked.

"Far end of town," Murphy said. "In fact, it's barely in town."

"Then let's get over there."

"Wait," Caleb said, "the sheriff can't go."

"Why not?"

"Because his badge would be a target in there," Caleb said.

"He's right," Murphy said. "They'd just as soon shoot me as look at me in there. You'll have to go."

"Okay," Clint said.

"I'll go in with you," Caleb said.

"Just take me there, Caleb," Clint said. "I'll go in and see if Bowen is there."

"Alone?"

"Don't worry," Clint said. "How many friends has Bowen got?"

"None," Caleb said, "but the men in that place will back him against you."

"Will they?"

"Well . . . they'd back him against any lawman."

"I'm not a lawman," Clint said, "am I?"

Caleb and Murphy took Clint to the edge of town and beyond—again—where a building sat alone, lit up, but quiet.

"That's a saloon?" Clint asked.

"A place to drink," Caleb said, "or play cards. No music."

"Any girls?"

"No," Caleb said. "Girls would cause trouble."

"And whiskey? Beer? They don't cause trouble?"

"If they do," Caleb said, "Warden takes care of it. In his place he's judge and jury."

Clint looked at Murphy.

"Who is Warden?"

"He used to be a bounty hunter. He gave it up to run his saloon," Murphy said.

"This place?"

"Not this one," Caleb said. "He's had others, but they always go out of business."

"Then every time he reopens, the place gets worse and worse. This is pretty much the bottom of the barrel."

"Why doesn't he go back to bounty hunting?" Clint wondered.

"He's in his fifties now," Murphy said, "been out of the saddle for some time. I don't think that idea appeals to him."

"And this does?"

"Whatever it is," Murphy said, "it's his."

"All right, then," Clint said. "You two stay here. I'll go inside and see if Bowen is there."

"All right," Murphy said, "but at the first sign of trouble, I'm comin' in."

"I hope I won't need you."

He started toward the building, then stopped and looked at Caleb Stone.

"How will I know Warden?" he asked.

"You'll know him," Caleb said. "He's always behind the bar."

Clint nodded.

Close up, the building looked as if it would fall over with a good push. As he approached the front door, he could hear some voices from inside. The door was just a door, no batwings, just a wooden door with a doorknob. He turned it, and entered.

The interior was small, stuffy, filled with smoke. About a dozen tables were spread out before him, but only several were occupied. The men turned to look at him.

Clint looked at the bar. Behind it was a man in his fifties, bald on top with a fringe of hair, and a thoroughly unpleasant face that had seen the wrong end of a few rifle butts in its time.

No one in the place resembled Jess Bowen.

Clint walked to the bar, which was empty at the moment.

"What've you got on your mind, friend?"

"A beer."

The bartender laughed.

"And for that you came here? You got plenty of places to get beer in town."

"None of them have your . . . character."

"Hee-hee," one of the men at a table laughed. "Hey, Warden, this here feller thinks you got character." Then he stopped laughing and frowned. "What's that mean?"

"It means I want a beer," Clint said. "Why don't you shut up and mind your own business?"

"Take it easy, friend," Warden said. "Jerry's an idiot. Don't mind him. I'll get you a beer."

He drew one and set it in front of Clint. When he sipped it, he was pleasantly surprised to find that it was cold.

"That's good," he said.

"Not what you expected, eh?" Before Clint could answer, he went on. "That's okay. I know how this place looks to people."

"Are you the owner?" Clint asked.

"Yeah," the man said, then extended his hand. "Jay Warden. This is Warden's Saloon."

Clint shook his hand, surprised that the man was so friendly and forthcoming.

"What made you come wanderin' in here?" Warden asked.

"Well," Clint said, "I didn't actually wander in. I was sort of . . . sent here."

"By who?" Warden asked suspiciously. "And why?"

"I'm looking for someone."

"Who?"

"A man named Jess Bowen."

"The only reason I can think of for anyone to be lookin' for Jess Bowen is if he did somethin' to make you mad."

"Well . . . he might have killed somebody."

"Somebody you knew?"

"No," Clint said, "somebody else I needed to talk to."

"And who was that?"

"Willie Delvin."

Warden leaned his elbows on the bar.

"Jess killed Willie?"

"We think so."

"We?"

"The sheriff and me."

"Murphy?" Warden straightened up. "Is he outside?"

"Yes," Clint said. "So is Caleb Stone."

"Well," Warden said, "this just keeps gettin' better and better."

"What do you—"

"You better go out and bring them in," Warden said. "I'll get rid of these guys."

THIRTY-TWO

A few minutes later Clint, Murphy, Caleb Stone, and Jay Warden were seated at a table with a beer in front of each of them.

"Maybe you know more about Willie and Jess than the sheriff does," Clint said. "Were they friends?"

"Friends? No, not that I know of."

"Were you friends with either of them?" Clint asked.

"Can't say that either."

"Then what?"

Warden shrugged.

"I knew them, they knew each other. They had one thing in common."

"They'd do anythin' for money," Murphy said.

Warden nodded.

"That was it," Warden said, "but Jess, he'd go a lot further than Willie."

"Murder?" Clint asked.

"Jess likes to kill," Warden said. "He prefers to do it for money, though."

"Whose money?" Clint asked.

"Anybody's."

Caleb was the first to finish his beer.

"Can I have another one?" he asked.

"No," Murphy said.

"Look, Mr. Warden," Clint said, "Caleb, here, is supposed to help us find Jess Bowen."

"Bowen'll kill him," Warden said. "I mean, if you're right and he killed Willie, he ain't gonna wanna be found."

"So tell me," Clint said. "Where does Bowen go when he doesn't want to be found?"

"What makes you think I know that?" Warden asked.

"Because you asked us to come inside and you closed up," Clint said. "That means you didn't want anybody knowing you talked to us."

Warden studied Clint for a few seconds, then drank some beer before talking.

"Okay," he said, "this is what I heard. There's a town about twenty miles from here called Ferguson."

"Ferguson?" Clint looked at Murphy, who scowled.

"Ferguson is a ghost town," the lawman said.

"That's right," Warden said. "There's nobody there. That's just how a man like Jess Bowen likes it."

"That's where he hangs his hat?" Murphy asked.

"I told you," Warden said. "It's somethin' I heard."

"Well," Clint said, "it's more than we had before." He looked at Murphy. "I'll take a ride out there tomorrow. It's not that far."

"Especially not on that horse of yours," Murphy said.

"What am I supposed to do?" Caleb asked.

"You?" Murphy said. "You're gonna spend the night in one of my cells."

"What? Why?"

"Because we don't want anybody tellin' Bowen that Clint is lookin' for him."

"I ain't gonna tell nobody."

Murphy stood up, slid his hand beneath Caleb's arm, and lifted the man to his feet.

"We're just gonna make sure of that," the lawman said. He looked at Clint. "You comin'?"

"I'm going to finish my beer, and then turn in."

"Well, stop by the office in the mornin', before you head for Ferguson."

"I'll do that."

As Murphy left with Caleb, Warden asked, "You want a fresh one?"

"Sure."

Warden went to the bar and came back with two fresh beers.

"Why you hangin' around here now?" he asked.

"I'm just wondering if there's something you might want to tell me that you didn't want to say in front of the sheriff."

"Like what?"

Clint shrugged.

"I don't know. You tell me."

"Well, I'll tell you somethin' I been thinkin' about lately, Adams."

"What's that?"

"Comin' outta retirement."

"As a bounty hunter, you mean?"

"That's right," Warden said. "And I could use a partner."

"Me?"

"I can't think of a better partner than the Gunsmith," Warden said. "Who better to watch my back?"

"I'm flattered," Clint said, "but I'm no bounty hunter."

"So what are you?" Warden asked. "The killer everybody says you are?"

"I'm not anything other people think I am," Clint said.

"And don't you want to prove that?"

"To who?" Clint asked. "I know who I am, and I don't need to prove it to anyone else."

"I tell you what," Warden said. "Let me ride with you to

Ferguson. If, by the time we get back, you don't wanna team with me, I'll forget about it and stop askin'."

"Why would I need you to come to Ferguson with me?" Clint asked. "Isn't it a ghost town?"

"Just because it's a ghost town doesn't mean there's nobody there," Warden said.

"I hope to find Jess Bowen there."

"Yeah, but he might not be alone."

"What are you saying?" Clint asked. "That Ferguson is a haven for other men like Bowen?"

"Exactly."

"And why didn't you tell me that in front of the sheriff?" Clint asked.

"Because," Warden said, "then he woulda wanted to go with you."

THIRTY-THREE

Early the next morning Clint rode Eclipse to the sheriff's office, dismounted, and went inside.

"Ready to go?" Murphy asked.

"Just about. Where's Caleb?"

"In a cell," Murphy said, "still asleep."

"Good," Clint said. "Keep him there a little bit longer. Better yet, until we get back."

"We?"

"Yes," Clint said. "Warden's coming with me."

"Warden? Why?"

"According to him," Clint explained, "Bowen may not be alone in Ferguson."

"I thought he didn't have friends."

"Not friends," Clint said, "just colleagues, sort of."

"You mean, there might be other men there who don't want to be found?"

"Exactly."

"Other wanted men?" Murphy asked. "Maybe I should come with you, after all."

"No, no," Clint said. "You can go to Ferguson another time. Let me do what I have to do first."

"Okay," Murphy said, "agreed."

Clint heard a horse outside and said, "I better get going."

Outside the office, Clint found Jay Warden waiting for him astride a painted pony that had seen better days.

"That's your horse?" he asked.

"Has been for a long time," Warden said. "Silvertip and me, we hunted plenty of outlaws together."

"You think this horse can keep up with mine?"

Warden grinned.

"Wait and see."

Clint mounted up and said, "Why wait?"

Several miles outside of town Clint reined Eclipse in and waited for Warden to catch up.

"Okay," Warden said, "the old boy can't keep up."

"On the contrary," Clint said. "I'm very impressed with him. Eclipse would have outdistanced most horses by now. Yours kept you close."

"Even so," Warden said, "can we proceed at a little bit more . . . reasonable pace?"

"I think that can be arranged," Clint said.

They rode on ahead, abreast this time.

They came to a sign that said FERGUSON, with the population number crossed out and replaced several times. Apparently, somebody decided it was time to stop, because the sign was lying on the ground.

"The town is just up the road there, around the bend," Jay Warden said.

"Have you been here before?"

"Once," Warden said. "It was my last bounty. I found the fella here."

"So what are we looking at?"

"A collection of buildings that look like they're gonna fall down," Warden said. "Honestly, some of them probably have since the last time I was here. Bowen could be there alone, he could be there with some other fellas—or he might not be there at all."

"Anybody there going to know you from your old profession?" Clint asked.

"Are you worried that we might get shot at as soon as we ride in?"

"I am."

"Well, I don't think anybody's gonna know me," Warden said, "but somebody might know you and take a shot at you."

"That's always a risk with every town I ride into," Clint told him. "If that's all we have to worry about, we might as well just go ahead and ride in."

"It's your call," Warden said.

They rode forward together.

THIRTY-FOUR

As they rode down the main street of Ferguson—or what used to be the town of Ferguson—Clint saw what Warden meant. Many of the buildings had already fallen in on themselves to some degree. Some had half a roof, others three walls, still others had boarded-up windows.

There was nobody on the street, and not a sound from anywhere. They reined in their horses in front of a deserted-looking saloon. They dismounted, Warden tying his horse to a hitching rail, Clint simply wrapping Eclipse's reins once around it with a flick of his wrist.

"Too quiet," Clint said. "Somebody's watching us."

"I know," Warden said. "I can feel it."

Clint looked at him.

"The old instincts don't die."

"I hope not," Clint said. "Let's go inside."

"What about the horses?" Warden asked. "We don't need somebody takin' them."

"My horse won't go with anyone," Clint said. "He'll sound the alarm."

"Smart animal."

"The smartest."

"Okay, then."

They mounted the boardwalk and entered the saloon. As they did, one of the batwing doors fell off its hinges.

"Let's hope the rest of the building doesn't follow," Clint said.

Inside they found dust, bits and pieces of what used to be tables and chairs. There were, however, a couple of tables and four chairs at each. Clint walked to them and ran his finger over them.

"No dust," he said, showing Warden his fingertip.

"I see. I'll check the bar."

Warden walked to the bar, and around it.

"Got some glasses here that have been used recently," he said. "And some whiskey bottles."

"Are there any other saloons in town?"

"No," Warden said. "You can see how small this town is. This is the one saloon."

Clint looked around.

"We may have made a mistake coming in here."

Across the street, in what used to be the hardware store, Jess Bowen watched from the window as Clint and Jay Warden entered the saloon.

"They're inside," he told the others.

"Then we have them," one of the other men said.

"Let's don't be in a hurry," Bowen said. He pointed. "You two get up on the roof." Pointed again. "You two outside, on either side of this storefront. Nobody fires unless I do. Understood?"

They all nodded.

"Go!"

That left one man with him.

"We gonna get this done?" Andy Cardwell asked.

Bowen looked at the whorehouse bouncer, whose sole reason for wanting to kill the Gunsmith was jealousy, and said, "That's what I'm gettin' paid for."

* * *

"What are you thinkin'?" Warden asked.

"I'm thinking we should stay away from the windows, for one thing."

"You wanna go out the back?"

"No," Clint said.

"But if they're waitin' out front to ambush us—"

"If they are," Clint interrupted him, "it means we know where they are. If we go out the back, then we're acting blind, still looking for them."

"You keep saying 'them,'" Warden said. "You're convinced there's more than one?"

"I doubt Jess Bowen would act alone."

Warden was still behind the bar, so he leaned his elbows on it, a familiar and comfortable position.

"I can read your mind," he said.

"Can you?" Clint pulled a chair away from one of the tables and sat down. "Tell me."

"You're thinkin' this was a trap," Warden said. "That we were lured here for Bowen to take."

"Not we," Clint said. "Me."

"That would mean that whoever told you about this place was in on the plan. Or at least, one of the people who knew you were comin' here."

"Probably."

"So that would mean it's either Caleb, the sheriff—"

"Or you," Clint finished.

"And what's your best guess?" Warden asked.

"I say it was you," Clint said.

"Oh yeah? Why's that?"

"You insisted on coming with me," Clint said. "And you fed me that manure about wanting to come out of retirement with me as your partner."

Warden fidgeted a bit behind the bar, moving one hand.

"And I'm willing to bet Bowen left a shotgun under that bar for you."

Warden stopped moving his hand.

"You're crazy."

"Am I? There's two ways to tell."

"Howzat?"

"Either you pull that shotgun out and take your chance . . ." Clint said.

"Or?" Warden asked.

"Or I walk over there and take a look. If there's shotgun there, I'll kill you."

THIRTY-FIVE

"Your choice," Clint said.

Clint thought the ex–bounty hunter looked nervous. He'd been away from this kind of thing a long time.

"You're crazy," Warden said again.

"Well then," Clint said, "get out from behind there so I can take a look."

Warden didn't move, but Clint saw his eyes flick to the big window in front of the saloon.

Across the street Jess Bowen sighted down the barrel of his rifle. Through the front window of the saloon he could see the bar, and Jay Warden, but the ex–bounty hunter was not his target.

Not yet anyway.

"All right, Adams," Warden said. "I'll move, and you can see how wrong you are."

The big man took his hands off the bar, turned as if to walk around it, then suddenly snatched the shotgun from beneath the bar and tried to bring it to bear.

But Clint was expecting it. He drew and fired once, drilling the man through the chest. His eyes went wide, his hands opened, and the shotgun fell to the floor. Seconds later, so did he.

Clint ejected the spent shell and replaced it before doing anything else. He thought he was going to need all six. Then he moved to the bar, crouched down by the prone man, who—for the moment—was still breathing.

"What am I looking at, Warden?" he asked. "What am I facing out there? How many?"

Warden's eyes were wide and glassy, as if he was doing all he could to keep them open and stay alive.

"Am I—am I—" he stammered.

"Dying. Yeah, you're dying. So tell me what I need to know," Clint said. "How many?"

For a moment Clint thought he wasn't going to get any help from the dying man. He either wouldn't, or couldn't, say anything, but then he took a deep breath, gasped out the word, "Six," and died.

"Come on, Adams," Bowen said, still sighting down his gun barrel. "Make it easy. Stand up."

He'd seen Warden go down, and had a split second of Clint Adams before the man ducked down behind the bar. Now he was waiting for Adams to stand back up.

"Stand up, you sonofabitch."

Clint started to stand up, then remembered the window. Warden had risked a glance at it for a reason. So he crawled out from behind the bar and didn't stand still until he was away from the window, out of sight of anyone looking in, maybe from across the street. Window, rooftop, whatever.

Standing in the back of that saloon, he knew what he'd gotten himself into—maybe knew it even when he first left the town of Chester to come to Ferguson with Jay Warden.

The question now was, what to do?

* * *

Across the street Jess Bowen knew things had gone wrong—
maybe terribly wrong.

Adams should have stood up behind the bar by now, if
he was going to.

"You better get the men back here," he said to Cardwell.

"What for?"

Bowen turned around and looked at the man.

"It's not goin' as planned," he said.

"So what are we doin'?"

"We're goin' in."

He decided.

If they were outside waiting for him to come out, they
were going to wait a long time.

Sitting back in a chair, he settled down to wait for them
to come in.

THIRTY-SIX

Clint decided to take a quick look around before settling down. He satisfied himself that there was no back door, no other way in but through a window. And he'd hear it if somebody broke one. The place was small, all on one level, so there was no upstairs to worry about.

He returned to the main part of the saloon, sat back down in his chair. From there he could see the front windows on either side of the batwing doors.

"How're we gonna do this?" Cardwell asked.

"Like I said," Bowen answered, "we're goin' in."

"Look," Cardwell said nervously, "I'm no gunman."

"That right?" Bowen asked. "You didn't say that when you said you wanted in on this. You said you wanted Adams dead. You think I'm just gonna do that job for you outta the goodness of my heart?"

"Well, no, but—"

"Then get ready," Bowen said. "We're goin' in. You'll be with me."

"Yeah," Cardwell said, "okay."

"You two are goin' in first," he told the two men who had been on the roof.

"What?" one of them asked. "He'll shoot us as soon as we go through the door."

"That's why you ain't gonna go through the door," Bowen said. "Yer goin' in through the windows."

The two men looked at each other.

Clint once again crawled behind the bar and grabbed the shotgun. He should have thought to take it with him the first time. Now he had his Colt and the shotgun, an over-and-under Greener.

He checked it, found it fully loaded. He had no other shells, so he'd have to make these two count.

For a third time he settled down in his chair. He kept his breathing steady, kept himself as relaxed as he could, considering what he was facing. There were six men coming for him, but at least he knew they had to come in the front.

What they didn't have to do was come in the front door . . .

Jess Bowen and his men left the storefront they were in and started across the street toward the saloon. Bowen kept a sharp eye out in case Adams was trying to peer out one of the front windows, but there was no sign of him. Apparently, the man had decided to stand his ground and wait for them to come in after him.

Well, that suited Bowen. His odds were six to one, and he'd take those odds anytime.

"There," he said, pointing to a window, "and there. On my signal."

The two men nodded and took up their position. They were getting paid enough for this.

"You two go right through the batwings as they go through the windows," Bowen said.

"Right."

Bowen looked at Cardwell.

"We go in after them."

Cardwell nodded nervously, licking his lips.

Jess Bowen drew his gun, then signaled his men with a wave of his arm.

The windows were both missing some of the glass, but it still made quite a racket as the two men came crashing through.

Expecting this move, Clint concentrated on the batwing doors. It would take the men who crashed through the windows a few seconds to regain their balance. As the other two men came through the door, he let go with both barrels of the shotgun.

The blast widened and took care of both men, driving them back out the doors and into the street.

The two men on the floor struggled to get to their feet, going for their guns. One of them found an empty holster, as his gun had fallen from it.

Clint fired at both men, dispatching them with great dexterity. If Warden had told him the truth before dying, that left two outside—Bowen and one other.

As the two men came flying through the batwing doors, landing in the street, Caldwell backed away, staring at their bloody forms.

"Jesus," he said.

"Damn it," Bowen said.

"What do we do?" Cardwell asked.

"Well," Bowen said, "we're not goin' in there. Let's get to the horses. We'll get him another time."

But Clint had other ideas . . .

Discarding the shotgun, bypassing the dead bodies, he ran for the batwing doors, hoping to catch the other two men unawares. As he came through the doors, he saw them in the street, just starting away from the saloon. The bigger man had to be Bowen. He recognized the other man as Cardwell, the man who worked at the whorehouse.

"Hold it!"

Both men stopped cold.

"Turn around."

Both men did. They still had their guns in their hands. Clint's gun was holstered.

"Don't do anything stupid," he said. "Your partners are dead."

"Don't—don't—" Cardwell stammered.

"Shut up!" Bowen said. "Whataya want, Adams?"

"I want to know who sent you after me," Clint said. "That's all. Who told you to kill Willie, and who sent you after me."

"I tell you that," Bowen said, "I don't get paid."

"If you force me to kill you, you don't get paid either."

"J-Jess . . ." Cardwell stammered.

"Settle down," the big man said without looking at him. "Don't panic."

But Cardwell had all the telltale signs of a man who was going to panic. He couldn't keep still, his eyes kept darting about, he was sweating and licking his lips. Clint knew if it was only Cardwell he had to worry about, there would be no problem. Even if the man tried to draw his gun, Clint knew he could wound him easily. But if Cardwell panicked and drew, then Bowen would have no choice but to draw also. In that case Clint would have no time to be fancy. He'd have to shoot to kill. He never liked shooting unless it was to kill, but he wanted to keep at least one of these men alive to talk to him.

"Look, Bowen," Clint said, "just tell me what I want to know and you can ride out."

"And go where?" Bowen asked. "I took a job and I gotta do it. If I don't, I'll never get another one."

"Like I said," Clint told him, "if you make me kill you, it's over. You won't need another job."

THIRTY-SEVEN

Over breakfast in their house, Veronica Perryman wanted to know what was going on.

"With what?" Perryman asked.

"Don't play games with me, Milton," she said. "Clint Adams and the boy."

"They're being taken care of."

"How?"

He put his silverware down and stared at her.

"Veronica, since when do I discuss my business affairs with you?" he asked.

"This is not just your business, Milton," she said. "This is our lives. If that little boy lives, then he's the rightful heir to all of this."

"How is anybody going to know that with my brother and his family dead?" Perryman asked.

"But his family isn't dead," she said. "Not all of them."

"There's no one left back East, Veronica," Perryman said. "No one who can testify to the fact that there's another heir."

"Not another heir," she said. "The heir. You stole all this from your brother, and he was coming to take it back. When you had him killed, his son became the rightful heir."

Perryman pounded his fist on the table. The cook came rushing out of the kitchen, thinking he wanted her.

"It's all right, Molly," he said, waving at her. "Go back into the kitchen."

When the cook was gone, Veronica said, "Milton, you need to talk to me."

"I think what we need to do, Veronica," he said, standing up, "is go upstairs. You need a lesson."

"You wouldn't dare."

He walked around the table, a raging erection pulsing almost painfully in his pants. He grabbed her arm, dragged her from the dining room, and up the stairs.

Bowen was the gunhand, but Clint kept his eyes on Cardwell. He was the one who was going to call the play.

"Bowen, your friend is going to do the wrong thing."

"I did the wrong thing," Bowen said. "I should've killed you when you rode in."

Clint was about to reply, but Cardwell seemed to take that statement as a signal. He went for his gun.

"Don't—" Clint started to yell, but it was too late. Bowen knew what was happening and he also went for his gun.

Clint had no choice.

He drew and fired, hitting Bowen first, because he was now the danger. Cardwell was so panicked he almost dropped his gun. When he finally started to bring it to bear, Clint shot him once in the chest.

He rushed to both fallen men, hoping that at least one of them was still alive and, if so, that he'd be the one who could answer his questions.

No such luck.

Both men were dead.

"Damn!"

He stood, ejected the spent shells, replaced them, and put his gun back in his holster, looking around. The town was quiet. Either there was no one there, or no one else wanted any part of this.

He walked to Eclipse, mounted up, and rode out before anyone could change his mind.

Perryman pulled Veronica into their bedroom and slammed the door. She was still wearing her nightgown and robe from the night's sleep.

"Milton—"

He growled, reached out, and tore the robe and gown from her body. Her full breasts bobbed into view, their brown nipples already distended. He could see—could smell—that she was as aroused as he was. Teaching her a lesson was always one of his—one of their—favorite things.

"Milton . . ." she said warningly.

He backhanded her across the face, knocking her onto the bed, legs going wide. Her pubic hair glistened with her wetness. She stared at him, wiped her mouth with the back of her hand, stared at the blood there.

"All right, then," she said. "Come ahead."

Clint rode until he was well past the fallen FERGUSON sign, then stopped and looked back. No one was following him. If there were more men in that dead town, they had minded their own business—and were still doing so.

He urged Eclipse into a gallop. He wanted to get back to Chester as soon as possible.

He tore off his own clothes and stood there naked. Although ten years older than she was, he was still a fine figure of a man, tall, fit, and virile.

"Come on, come on," she said, moving back on the bed. "We don't have all day."

"You talk too much," he said.

She smiled at him.

"Then put something in my mouth to shut me up."

When he reached the bed, he grabbed her ankles and pulled her off, onto the floor. He then lifted her to her knees, grabbed her head, and forced his rigid cock into her mouth. She snorted, but took it and began to suck it.

"That's my good girl," he said soothingly.

"Mmmm," she said, sliding him in and out of her mouth, wetting him thoroughly, then pausing to lick him before taking him in once again.

THIRTY-EIGHT

When Clint rode back into Chester, he went directly to Sheriff Murphy's office. He entered without knocking. Murphy looked up in surprise, settled back when he saw it was Clint.

"What happened?"

"It was a trap," Clint told him. "They were waiting for me. Bowen and some men."

"What happened to Warden?"

"He's dead," Clint said. "He was in on it. I had to kill him, too."

"Too?"

"Yes," Clint said. He walked to the stove, poured himself a cup of coffee, and then sat down. "I had to kill all of them," he said after a swallow.

"Bowen?"

"Him, too."

Murphy scowled.

"Did you get any information?"

"No," Clint said. "Nothing."

"So we're back where we started."

Clint thought for a moment before answering.

"Maybe."

"Why maybe?"

"Who has enough money to arrange that kind of thing?" Clint asked. He sat forward, warming to his subject. "To pay six men to kill me?"

"Well . . ." Murphy said, giving it a moment's thought. "A few people, actually—".

Clint shook his head.

"But somebody that I've already met."

"Well . . . Perryman, and maybe the mayor."

"Not the mayor," Clint said.

"Why not?"

"I don't think he would risk something like that this close to the election."

"So that leaves Perryman."

"Right."

"But you can't prove it," Murphy said. "Nobody talked to you in Ferguson."

"That may be," Clint said, "but Perryman doesn't know that, does he?"

"You plannin' on bluffin' him?"

"Sometimes," Clint said, "a bluff is your only play."

"How are you going to work it?"

"I don't know yet."

"When will you know?"

Clint thought about it for a moment, then said, "After my next cup of coffee."

Murphy got up and said, "Or maybe I should make another pot."

Veronica Perryman needed a bath after her husband left her naked on their bed, bruised and thoroughly fucked. He always felt he was teaching her a lesson when he treated her this way, but she liked her sex rough. On the rare occasion when they did have sex, it went this way. One day he might even kill her. Or the other way around.

She luxuriated in the bath, the hot water easing her aches and, possibly, her tension. She didn't want anyone taking her husband's fortune away before she could get her hands on it. When they first heard that Milton's brother had found out about his inheritance, and was coming with his family, she'd panicked. But she had to give her husband credit— he'd remained calm and come up with a plan. The only thing that had gone wrong was that boy getting away.

They had never had children of their own. For a brief moment she had thought of taking the child in, raising him themselves. Then he would be an heir, one way or the other, only he would be Milton's heir. But Milton wouldn't hear of that plan. He wanted the child dead.

She had to give her husband credit. He never shied away from doing what had to be done.

She took her sponge, rubbed it between her legs, her head back on the edge of the tub. Sex didn't always have to be rough for her. Sometimes she liked it soft.

And sometimes she liked it by herself . . .

Perryman went back down to the dining room when he was finished with his wife. He didn't need a bath. After he had taught his wife a lesson, he liked to have her stink on him all day, to remind him. Even when he was with a whore, he liked having the stink of his wife on him—and then the stench of both women.

He poured himself another cup of coffee, wondered if he'd be hearing from Jess Bowen that day. If the plan had gone as Bowen had mapped out, the big man should be back before dark. If not, if he took longer, his fee was going to go down— drastically.

"Molly!"

The cook appeared at the door. She was a woman in her late forties, a handsome woman who had once been beautiful. Before he married his wife and brought her to his house, he used to fuck Molly. Afterward, he kept her on as his cook.

"Yes, sir?" she asked, wiping her hands on her apron. "Do you want something else to eat?"

"No. Tell my wife I went to town."

"Will you be back for supper?"

"I'll be eating at the Crystal."

"All right," she said. "I'll tell her."

"See that you do."

He turned and left the room. Moments later Molly heard the front door close. She looked at his empty coffee cup. Maybe at the Crystal they'd finally do what she didn't have the courage to.

Poison him.

THIRTY-NINE

By the time they finished the new pot of coffee, Clint thought he had a plan.

"That's how you want to play it?" Murphy asked him.

"I can't think of another way," Clint said. "Every time we think we've got somebody to talk to, they end up dead."

"Well," Murphy said, "it was you who killed them this time."

"I told you I didn't have a choice."

"I know, I know," Murphy said. "But hittin' Perryman head on with this—"

"How do you think he'll react?"

"He'll send some more men after you," Murphy said. "This time enough to do the job."

"Or maybe," Clint said, "enough so that I can keep at least one of them alive."

"And then you've got to get him to talk," Murphy said. "You might have better luck tryin' to get somebody inside the house to talk."

"Wait a minute," Clint said, "what?"

"I said you might have more luck—"

"How many other people live in his house?"

"At least three," Murphy said, "all women. His wife, his housekeeper, and his cook."

"And these three women," Clint asked, "are they loyal to him?"

"Well," Murphy said, "to the best of my recollection, they all hate his guts."

"Oh, Murphy," Clint said, "this is something you should have told me before . . ."

Now that Clint knew there were three people inside Milton Perryman's house who might know what was going on, he had himself a new plan. But first he had to determine where Perryman was for the day.

"The easiest way to do that is to check the Crystal Chandelier," Murphy said. "That's pretty much a club for the cattlemen. He drinks there, eats there, and . . . well, pretty much does everythin' else there."

"Everything else?" Clint asked. "You mean, girls?"

"Yeah, that, too."

"And where does he get the girls from?"

"Where else?" Murphy asked. "Maddy's."

"Sheriff," Clint said, "the longer we talk, the more information I find you have to give me."

"Well," Murphy complained, "ya never asked me before—"

"I'm asking you now," Clint said, cutting him off. "Do you have anything else to tell me? Anything helpful?"

Murphy thought a moment, then said, "No, I ain't."

"So there's a whole other way for me to go after Milton Perryman," Clint said.

"And how's that?"

"Women!"

Clint left the sheriff's office and went to Maddy's. One of the girls let him in and took him to Lily's office.

"Here to see me," she asked with a saucy smile, "or our boy?"

"Your man Cardwell is dead."

She looked shocked.

"What?"

"Dead."

"How?"

"I killed him."

"Okay," she said after a moment, "why?"

"He tried to kill me."

"Again," she said, "why?"

"Over you, I suppose," he said, "but he aligned himself with another man, who was hired to kill me."

"At the risk of repeating myself," she said, "why?"

"Why did he align himself, or why was a man hired to kill me?" he asked.

"Well . . . both."

"I assume the man was hired because of the boy," Clint said. "Because I'm trying to find out who killed his family."

She sat back in her chair and looked exhausted.

"I'm going to stop asking questions, and you just go on talking."

"How about I ask you some questions?"

"Go ahead."

"Do you know Milton Perryman?"

"Everyone knows Perryman."

"No, I mean, do you know him personally?"

"Well, yes."

"Does he come here?"

"Did you ask me these questions before?"

"I don't know," Clint said. "Can you answer them now?"

She sighed and said, "No, he doesn't come here. I send girls to him at the Crystal."

"Girls," Clint asked, "or a particular girl?"

"Well," she said, "when she's available, he likes Neve."

"Neve?" Clint said. "Have I met her?"

"No."

"What does he like about her?"

"Well," Lily said, "the main thing is she's sturdy, and doesn't mind being roughed up."

"Roughed up?" Clint said. "You mean . . . beaten?"

"You might call it that," Lily said, "but she doesn't mind as long as he pays for the privilege."

"Do you know if he does the same thing to his wife?"

"I don't know for sure," she said, "but I imagine he does. I mean, why wouldn't he, if it's what he likes?"

"Sounds right," Clint said.

"Why are you interested in Perryman?"

"I think he had the boy's family killed."

"But why?"

"That's what I want to find out," Clint said. "So far every man who might have helped me is dead."

"So . . . you're going to start talking to women?"

"That's right."

"Starting with Neve."

"Yes."

"And then Mrs. Perryman?"

"Yes," he said. "What do you know about her?"

"He went to California on business about ten years ago and came back with her."

"Do you know her?"

"Just in passing. She rarely comes to town, and when she does, she shops."

"And there are other women in the house?"

"His housekeeper and his cook," she said. "Only the cook was more than that until he brought his wife home."

"But now she's only the cook? Why does she stay?"

"He pays her well."

"I guess he pays all the women in his life well to endure his abuse," Clint said.

"Somebody should put a stop to it."

"Maybe that's what I'll do," Clint said. "What's his wife's name?"

"Veronica."

"And the cook?"

"Molly O'Brien."

"And the housekeeper?"

"Katy Olson."

"Do you know them?"

"Like Veronica," she said, "in passing."

"All right," Clint said. "Is Neve here?"

"Yes."

"Can I see her?"

"She's upstairs in her room," Lily said. "I'll bring her down here."

"Why here?" he asked. "I can go to her room."

"No."

"Why not?"

"Because if you go to Neve's room, you'll end up fucking her," she said. "Or she'll fuck you."

"No I wo—"

"You won't have much of a choice, I'm afraid," Lily said, getting up from her desk. "That's the kind of girl she is. The effect she has on men."

"You don't think I'll be able to control myself?"

"Sure you will," she said, "but I'll bring her here and stay in the room anyway. Just to keep her from raping you."

"Lily—"

"Sit," she said, pushing him into a chair and then kissing him. "I'll be right back with her."

FORTY

About ten minutes later Lily returned to the office with Neve. He saw what Lily meant. She was a solidly built girl, what some men would even call meaty. She had a mass of red hair, big round breasts, and solid hips, and in the nightgown she was wearing she showed lots of freckled cleavage. She reeked of sex, and he could feel himself responding to it.

"Neve, this is Clint," Lily said.

"Well, hello," the big girl said.

"And he's mine," Lily added, "so just answer his questions and keep your hands off."

"Keep *my* hands off?"

"Never mind," Lily said. She leaned against the wall and folded her arms.

"You're stayin'?" Neve asked.

"Just answer the man's questions."

Neve turned to face Clint and folded her arms beneath her breasts, causing them to swell and almost fall out of her gown.

"What's on your mind, handsome?"

"Milton Perryman."

"One of my best customers."

"I understand he beats you."

She hesitated, then said, "He gets a little handsy some-times. But like I said, he's one of my best customers. What's this about?"

"The little boy I brought here a few days ago."

"Oh, him," she said. "What a doll."

"Yes, he is," Clint said. "I'm trying to find out who killed his family."

"You think Milton had somethin' to do with it?"

"Yes."

She stared at him for a few moments, then said, "Well, I suppose it had to happen."

"What's that?"

"That someone would ask."

"You mean, you know something about this?"

She hesitated again, then said, "Yes, I do."

"Then why haven't you told anyone?"

"I told you," she said, "he's my best customer."

"Neve—" Lily said.

Neve whirled on her boss and said, "Well, nobody asked me!"

"I'm asking you now, Neve," Clint said. "Do I need to ride out to Perryman's house and talk to his wife?"

"She wouldn't be able to tell you a thing," Neve said.

"But you can."

"Yes."

"Then do it, Neve," Lily said. "Start talkin'."

Clint stood up and motioned for Neve to take his chair. He perched a hip on the desk and said, "Go."

FORTY-ONE

Neve told Clint what she knew, what she had heard Milton Perryman say while in the throes of—well, not passion, but lust. She then told her story again to Sheriff Murphy, in his office.

"He was pretty stupid to say those things while he was with you," Murphy observed.

"Why?" she asked. "To him I'm just a whore. He didn't even think I was listening. I'm like a table or a chair to him."

"So let me get this straight," Murphy said. "He heard from a brother in the East who said he was coming west to claim what was his? That some uncle of theirs had willed the ranch to this brother, but the papers had been lost until now?"

"That's what he was muttering," Neve said. "He said how dare Henry want to come take what was his, meaning Milton's."

"And did he say what he was going to do about it?"

"He said he was going to take care of it," she said. "The way he takes care of everything—permanently."

"And you thought he meant by killing his own brother?"

"And his family."

"And he would do that?" Murphy asked.

"He would have it done by someone else," she said. "He's done it before."

"Maybe," the sheriff said, "we should talk about that, too."

"Some other time, Sheriff," Clint said. "I want to act on this information now."

"And do what?" Murphy asked.

"Arrest Perryman."

"On what evidence?"

"What Neve just told us."

"Clint," Murphy said, "that's just her opinion about what Perryman meant."

"What else could he have meant?"

"I don't know," Murphy said, "maybe he meant to buy his brother off."

"You really believe that?"

"No," Murphy said, "I don't, but I can't act unless I have evidence."

"All right, then," Clint said. "I'll just have to get you some evidence."

"Am I done?" Neve asked. "Since it looks like I'm going to lose my best customer, I should get back to work."

"I'll walk you back," Clint said.

"That's all right," she said to him. "Unless you're going to be my first customer today, I can find my own way back. You have your own work to do."

Both men watched her walk to the door and leave.

"That's quite a woman," Murphy said.

"Yes, she is."

"If Perryman is her best customer," the lawman said, "why would she be tellin' us these things about him?"

"I was wondering that myself," Clint said.

"Maybe she just wants to do the right thing."

"Maybe she does," Clint said, but he had his doubts.

* * *

Neve left the sheriff's office and hurried over to the Crystal. All the men in the place watched as she walked to Milton Perryman's table.

"Is it done?" he asked her.

"It's done."

He handed her a sheaf of bills and said, "Good job, honey."

"You get what you pay for," she told him, then left.

Perryman looked at the men around him. There were ten of them, lounging about, looking like customers.

"Get ready, men," he said. "The Gunsmith will be here soon."

They were all ready for the Gunsmith, because they were being paid enough to be ready.

"You ain't gonna march over to the Crystal, are ya?" Murphy asked. "That's Perryman's home away from home."

"No," Clint said, "I'm no fool. I'm thinking that's just what he wants me to do. Walk in the front door of the Crystal."

"I figured."

"So I'm not going to do that."

"Good, I thought maybe—"

"You are."

Murphy stopped short, then said, "Me?"

"But first I'm going to send a couple of telegrams."

FORTY-TWO

At the Crystal, Milton Perryman was wondering what the holdup was—and he wasn't the only one.

"What's takin' so long, boss?" Ed Lane asked. Lane was another gunman Perryman used for special jobs, and it was Lane who had collected all the other men on such short notice.

"It doesn't matter how long it takes, Ed," Perryman said. "He'll be here."

"Okay," Lane said, "you're the boss." And he went back to the bar.

But Perryman didn't like the fact that it was taking this long. He was glad he'd decided to wear a gun on this day. It added one more weapon to his arsenal.

Clint went to the telegraph office and sent two telegrams, then waited at the sheriff's office with Murphy until the replies came in.

"You really think you're gonna get answers today?" the lawman asked.

"I do," Clint said. "The men I sent the telegrams to are good friends of mine. They'll reply as quickly as they can."

He'd sent telegrams to Talbot Roper, who was a detective

in Denver, and also to Rick Hartman in Labyrinth, Texas, on the off chance that Roper was away on a job. He figured one of them would get him the information he needed.

It took two hours, but in the end, both men sent him the answer he was waiting for.

The clerk brought him both replies and Clint read them while Murphy looked on.

"Well?" Murphy asked.

"Confirmation that a man named Henry Perryman left Philadelphia with his wife and two children—Adele and Henry Junior—to come to Chester, Wyoming."

"Did they say why?"

"Apparently all the man said was he was going to visit family."

"So we have someone back there who can verify that the boy is part of that family?"

"Somebody," Clint said. "Not a family member, because there are no more, but a lawyer who knew the family."

"But that still don't give us any evidence," Murphy said.

"We're going to go and get us what we need right now, Sheriff," Clint said.

"Evidence?"

"Maybe," Clint said, "maybe not. But it'll be what we need. Are you ready?"

"To walk into the Crystal and go against Milton Perryman and his guns right there in his own club? I must be crazy, Adams. If it was anybody else but you, I wouldn't be ready, but God help me . . ."

He walked to the gun rack on the wall, took down a shotgun, then said, "Now I am."

FORTY-THREE

Sheriff Murphy wasn't at all sure that what he was doing was right. He knew it wasn't smart, but when would he ever get another chance to stand with a legend?

It was getting dark as he walked down the street and stopped just outside the Crystal. He doubted that there would be any other ranchers in the place with Milton Perryman. None of them would risk their lives for someone who was basically a rival.

At least, he hoped not.

He waited across the street, giving Clint time to go around the back.

Clint stopped at the back door of the Crystal, tried it, and found it locked. Like most back doors, it gave when he put his shoulder to it. Once inside, he heard voices from the saloon, but not the kind you'd usually hear from a place like that at this time of night.

He had borrowed a second pistol from Murphy, and had it tucked into his belt. He worked his way down the hallway he was in. At the end of the hall was a doorway to the saloon. He peered in and saw Milton Perryman seated at a table, and ten—he counted—men standing around, or leaning on the bar.

They were waiting for him. He started to wonder if this was the wrong play, but it was too late. Any minute the sheriff would be coming through the batwings, and he couldn't leave him on his own.

He drew both guns.

It was time.

Murphy crossed the street and mounted the boardwalk. He peered over the batwings, counted the men inside before going in, didn't see Clint anywhere.

Perryman spotted Sheriff Murphy looking over the batwings. He wondered if the man was there for a reason, or if he was just making rounds.

"Lane," Perryman said.

The hired gun turned from the bar, away from his conversation, and looked at his boss.

Perryman inclined his head toward the batwings, and Lane looked that way, then nodded. He turned back to his partners.

Clint watched the byplay between Perryman and the man at the bar. He felt he had now correctly identified the gun in charge. At that moment Murphy stepped through the doors.

Murphy stepped in and stopped.

"Sheriff," Perryman said. "What brings you here tonight?"

Instead of answering the question, Murphy said, "Not very busy tonight for this place."

"No, it's not," Perryman said. "In fact, this is kind of a . . . private party."

Clint took that as his cue.

* * *

"Is this party meant for me?" he asked, stepping through the back doorway.

Perryman turned in his seat and looked at Clint. Lane and the other men all straightened up.

Sheriff Murphy lifted the barrel of the shotgun he had been carrying down by his leg.

"Easy, boys," he said.

Perryman looked back at the lawman.

"If you're taking sides, Sheriff," he said, "you better be sure you make the right choice."

Murphy pointed the shotgun right at the rancher.

"If we're talkin' about decisions, Mr. Perryman," he said, "I think you better make the right one yourself."

FORTY-FOUR

Perryman held a staying hand out to Ed Lane and his boys.

"Let's talk, Mr. Perryman," Clint said.

Perryman looked at the guns in Clint's hands.

"At gunpoint?"

"Seems the safest way at the moment." Clint noticed that even Perryman himself was wearing a gun.

"What do you want to talk about, then?" Perryman asked.

"Let's start with your brother, Henry."

Perryman stiffened noticeably.

"What?"

"Your brother—"

"Who have you been talkin' to?" the rancher demanded.

"Why? Is there something I shouldn't know?"

Perryman didn't reply.

"Your brother was coming here with his wife, daughter, and little boy," Clint said. "Somebody headed them off and killed him, the wife, and the daughter, but the boy was left alive. I found him and brought him here, to Chester."

"You have the—" Perryman started, then stopped.

"Yes," Clint said, "I have the boy."

Perryman turned, looked at the sheriff, then at his men.

"You don't want these men to know you had your own

brother and his family killed?" Clint asked. "To protect your fortune?"

"That's not—" Perryman started.

"Or do some of them know that already?" Clint asked. "Yes, that's it, you've still got men out looking for the boy."

"Where is he?"

"He's safe," Clint said. "And he's going to want his money when he gets a little older, don't you think?"

"You can't prove—"

"I've got the word of a lawyer," Clint said, "who knows the family. That is, the family history."

Perryman's eyes flicked over to Ed Lane, who was watching Clint intently.

"Go ahead, Milton," Clint said. "Give him the word."

"These men will gun you and the lawman down," Perryman said.

"But not before we get some of them," Clint said, "oh, and you. You first, Milton. The sheriff still has his shotgun pointed right at you."

Perryman had been swiveling his head back and forth between Clint and the lawman.

"Why don't you stand up?" Clint asked.

"What?"

"Stand up so you can see better," Clint said. "And so you can get to that gun you're wearing."

Perryman stared at him.

"If you want some of these men to die for you, maybe you should be willing to put your own life on the line, as well." Clint looked at Lane, then some of the other men. "What do you boys think? Who wants to die for a man who killed his own family? And who wants to kill a two-year-old boy?"

Nobody answered. Ed Lane, though, had the eyes of a man who didn't care about any of that. He was getting paid to do a job.

"Sheriff, when they go for their guns, you blow a hole in Milton, and I'll take care of Ed Lane there." Clint looked at Lane. "You're the gunman, right? The rest of these men will follow your move?"

Lane stared at him.

"Well, make it!" Clint said. "One of you, make a move. Come on, Milton. Stand up!"

Milton Perryman stood up, but slowly put his hands in the air.

"You can't prove a thing," he said. "Not with my brother dead."

"That's okay, Milton," Clint said. "We've already got more than we had when we came in here. You just admitted to having a dead brother. What do you think, Sheriff?"

"I think Mr. Perryman's under arrest," Murphy said. "Unbuckle your gun belt and let it drop to the floor."

Perryman brought his hands down halfway, flexed his right hand, as if he wanted badly to go for his gun. Instead, he spoke to Lane.

"Are you and your men going to do something?" he demanded. "Kill them!"

One of the other men spoke.

"I didn't sign on to kill no lawman," he said. He started for the door, and some of the others followed. Then more.

"Lane!" Perryman said. "Kill Adams! Do it!"

"Yeah, come on, Lane," Clint said. "Do it." He holstered his Colt, stuck the other gun back in his belt. "I'll give you a fair shot at it."

"Drop your gun belt, Perryman," Murphy said. "I won't tell you again."

Reluctantly, the rancher undid his belt and let it drop.

"Now come with me," Murphy said. "You're under arrest."

"For what?"

"Conspiracy to commit murder."

"You can't prove that."

"I'll let a judge and a jury decide," Murphy said. "Meanwhile, I'm afraid your reputation will be a bit tarnished when all this comes out."

Perryman suddenly looked sorry he'd dropped his gun. Clint thought he might have preferred to go for the gun, rather than have the whole story be told.

"Come on."

Perryman walked to the doors, and out, followed by the sheriff. The other men had walked out, and were gone.

That left Lane and Clint in the saloon, and the bartender behind the bar.

"What's it going to be, Lane?" Clint asked.

The man stared at Clint for a few moments, then relaxed and said, "Maybe another time, Adams."

"Yeah," Clint said, "maybe."

FORTY-FIVE

"I'll take him."

"What?"

Lily was holding little Henry Perryman Jr., and his chubby arms were around her neck.

"I said I'll take him," she said. "I'll keep him."

"He may not see any of that Perryman money for a long time, you know," Clint warned her.

"I don't care about that," she said. "I just want to raise him."

"Why not?" Clint said. "I can't think of anyone better."

"You can't?" Lily asked. "You think this is a fit place to raise a kid?"

"I think you're a fit person to raise him," Clint said. "The place doesn't matter."

Clint looked at the newspaper on Lily's desk. The headline said, MILTON PERRYMAN ARRESTED FOR MURDER OF BROTHER. Whether it was true or not—though Clint was certain it was—Perryman's reputation was ruined.

"Do you really think that?" Lily asked.

"I do."

"Do you think I'll have any trouble?"

"You'll need to go before a judge," he warned her.

"Well," she said, "if it's the judge in this town, I shouldn't have too much of a problem."

"A customer?" he asked.

"A very good customer."

He kissed her, patted the little guy's head, and left.

Clint rode Eclipse over to the sheriff's office.

"Perryman's still in a cell," Murphy told him. "He'll go before the judge later today."

"The judge is going to be busy," Clint said.

"What?"

"Never mind," Clint said. "Do you need me?"

"No," Murphy said. "I was in the saloon with you, heard everything he said, and I've got that telegram you gave me from the lawyer back East. And . . . I've got a witness."

"What? Who?"

"Jason Kendall."

"Perryman's man?"

Murphy nodded.

"He came in early this mornin' and made a statement. He's hopin' to avoid jail time."

"Was he there?" Clint asked. "Did he kill them?"

"No," Murphy said, "well, he says no, but he says he knows who did it and he'll testify."

"Then you don't need me at all."

"No. You leavin' town today?"

"I am," Clint said. "Right now."

"What about the boy?"

"He's in good hands," Clint said, walking to the door. "He's in very good hands."